This Job Will Be The Death...

Victoria Hancox

This Job Will Be The Death….
The White-Collar Trilogy: Book 1

ISBN: 9798307670798

Text Copyright © Victoria Hancox 2025
All Rights Reserved
www.victoriahancox.com

Cover and interior artwork: AI generated

Introduction

Work, eh? Have you ever sat in a meeting that was so pointless, so boring and so long that you wondered whether you were trapped in Purgatory?
Yes? And if that was bad enough, how would you feel if you actually died and were forever bound to your office?
Welcome to *This Job Will Be the Death...* and your new corporate position.

You are playing as Ashley, who has found herself in the unfortunate position of being not only dead, but also permanently haunting the office. There's no clocking off! But can you unravel the mystery behind your untimely demise?

Playing is easy — you just do what you're told when you're told to! You do not read it as a conventional book but turn to the stated section number to continue the tale.

As there are many clues, codewords, objects and information to keep track of, the following pages contain the Record Sheets. Check them out but don't worry — apart from a little bit of calculations to keep your brain busy, you are just ticking boxes. Exactly like work...

Good luck!

Record Sheets

Clues

In any whodunnit, there are bound to be clues galore, but you can't solve a murder if you're busy trying to remember which ones you've found! Take a load off your mind by ticking the clues when instructed to.

1	☐	7	☐
2	☐	8	☐
3	☐	9	☐
4	☐	10	☐
5	☐	11	☐
6	☐	12	☐

Met-A-Ghost

Ghosts are funny things. Sure, when you're new, they'll materialise and chat, but when you want their help, they won't appear on demand. That's why it's important to make a note of **which ghosts you have already met**.

However, not every ghost that you meet needs to be recorded — just tick here when instructed to.

BEEHIVE GHOST ☐

CHARLIE ☐

CLARA ☐

MONICA ☐

NSFW GHOST ☐

PALE GHOST ☐

PARTY GHOST ☐

SCALPED GHOST ☐

Codewords

The choices you make at each stage will lead to a completely unique journey and to keep you on the right track, you will be told codewords. Tick them when instructed to.

CAUL ☐	**OPPORTUNITY** ☐
ECTOPLASM ☐	**OUIJA** ☐
LIMBO ☐	**PREMONITION** ☐
MEANS ☐	**TELEPORTATION** ☐
MIASMA ☐	**TREVOR** ☐

And if you need to convert a word into a number, then this might come in handy…

A	B	C	D	E	F	G	H	I	J	K	L	M
1	2	3	4	5	6	7	8	9	10	11	12	13
N	O	P	Q	R	S	T	U	V	W	X	Y	Z
14	15	16	17	18	19	20	21	22	23	24	25	26

Acquired Objects and Useful Information

As a rule of thumb, if something is **bold**, then it's probably important, and you should note it here.

The TRUTH About…

As time goes by, you will hopefully learn a thing or two about your former colleagues. Maybe you will even discover their deepest, darkest secrets…
When you have found out the **TRUTH about…** someone, you should tick their name here.

TRUTH about…

Adam ☐

Hannah ☐

Jan ☐

Louisa ☐

Marta ☐

Robert ☐

Theo ☐

PURGATORY Points

Throughout the saga, you will be instructed to add or subtract PURGATORY points, depending on your actions and their consequences.

You start with **ZERO** points, so may end with a negative or positive number.

You can keep a running tally here, but make sure that you know your final score — it will be crucial!

PURGATORY Points

Final Score:

Now, turn to the next page for the **Prologue**.

This Job Will Be The Death…

Prologue

Despite the darkness, you're able to recognise where you are. The office. But why are you here at night? By yourself? And then white smoke starts to swirl over the floorboards. Like dry ice, but it's not a concert or performance, so maybe it's a fire. The office is on fire. At night…

This is not making any sense, so you nod sagely and decide that it's just a dream. All you need to do is wake up, so you wait. And wait. And finally, a man in a suit and tie strolls in. You know him and so you should — you've worked with him for three years, but when you approach to say hello, he walks right through you. That's not good!

A snort of a laugh and waft of cigarette smoke alert you to the presence of a newcomer — a strange man perched on the edge of a desk. 'Strange' as in you don't know him, but also because he's wearing a distinctly Seventies gigantic-collared shirt. But at least he can see you, so you ask the obvious question:

  'Am I dead?'
  'Yes.'
  'Are you dead?'
  'Yes.'

This revelation that death isn't just a black pit of nothingness is quite novel and exciting; however, it is worrying that you're HERE in the office.

  'Is this Heaven or Hell or did I die here?'

There's no way he can give a monosyllabic response to that, so he stubs out his cigarette on the desk — an act that leaves no trace, although the living man does sniff the air with a perplexed look — then speaks.

'It's the in between place, and if you're here, it's because here is relevant for your death.'

You frown — that's about as clear as mud! — but he continues, 'I worked here and had a heart attack, but I died two days later in hospital. Whereas Clara was a maid and fell down the stairs, snapping her neck!'

She has your sympathy; those stairs are fearsomely steep. You've nearly come a cropper yourself—

'Oh! Is that how I died?'

'I don't know. I've got better things to do than sit around waiting for people to die!'

That plainly isn't true, but you're not going to argue with him right now.

'So why are you here? What unfinished business do you have?'

He stares daggers at you, then lights another cigarette before snapping, 'If I knew that I wouldn't be here. It's been long enough, at least a few months!'

Try five decades, you think, judging from his fashion and penchant for inside chain smoking, but wonder if time doesn't really matter now.

'I don't remember dying. Is that normal?'

'Can be, but that's usually the case when it's sudden or unexpected. You look young. Maybe you were murdered!'

And he puts a disturbingly excited stress on that last word, which isn't very sensitive, but what if he's right?

Well, the sad fact is that you seem to be stuck here, so you might as well do something useful. Why not find out the sorry story of your demise and, if foul play was the cause, perhaps you can get justice for yourself! Turn to **1**.

1

Abruptly, Chain-Smoking Ghost vanishes, which is an interesting trick, although you feel strangely abandoned and a little bit scared now.

'Hello!' you shout, but no one answers. The living man is now rooting around the drawers of the nearest desk, so to take your mind of the creeping loneliness, you decide to busy yourself with some fact finding, and this office is a good place to start.

Do you want to examine this nearby desk and see what the man is looking for (turn to **93**), go to the other desk (turn to **123**) or look out of the window (turn to **252**)?

2

So, you suspect that Robert was responsible for the curry. And his claim that he didn't say anything because he wanted to protect the alleged poisoner, Louisa, was just a cover-up. Something to shift attention away from the fact that he brought the poisoned food himself.

In that case, who was the intended victim? Who did Robert want to kill with the paracetamol overdose?

You	Turn to **91**
Hannah	Turn to **279**
Jan	Turn to **159**
Adam	Turn to **253**
Louisa	Turn to **52**
Theo	Turn to **134**
Marta	Turn to **5**

3

You peer over her shoulder, making her flinch and swat at an imagined insect, and read the first statement.

Speaks a second language fluently

You and Hannah both frown as you weigh up the possibilities. Who do you think Hannah should talk to first? Who do you think is bilingual?

Marta	Turn to **194**
Adam	Turn to **69**
Jan	Turn to **245**
Robert	Turn to **110**
Theo	Turn to **166**

4
You stamp around a bit more, but your heart isn't in it. Adam has practised a lifetime of denials and lies; he's not going to crack now. In fact, as the noise of your shoes abates, he wipes the tears from his face and announces to the room that he's going to set up a Facebook memorial page in your honour. You sigh and curse — silently, of course. You gave it your best shot, but you are stuck here now. Still, eternity can't last forever, can it…?

Your game ends here.

5
So, you think that Robert knew what Marta was doing and decided to kill her! Nice idea, but all the evidence points towards Robert having no knowledge of the thieving. In fact, he thought that the missing batch of Thunderbolt cables was his fault!

Add 5 PURGATORY points, then turn to **150**.

6

Maybe you have already found out who was in the office at the time of your murder; maybe you haven't, but there doesn't seem to be a lot more to do. You wander aimlessly around, hoping for inspiration, but what happens next is beyond what you could ever have expected! Turning right after the privacy pods, you stride down the narrow, plain corridor, only to see that, instead of the trendy exposed brickwork, there is now a door on your left!

'Well, that's not normally there,' you say, stating the obvious. You reach out to touch it — maybe it's just a hallucination — but you can feel the varnished wood under your fingertips.

If you have ticked the codeword ECTOPLASM and want to use this skill, turn to **297**. If you can't or won't open the door, then turn to **158**.

7

You grip the WLAN again and write, **'It is me. Who gave me the Thai curry?'**

Robert continues to stare, breathing rapidly through his gaping mouth.

'You were friends with my wife. Leave me alone,' he finally mutters — clearly unsettled — but if you're going to get anything out of Robert, you need to increase the fear factor. Have you acquired a pair of phantom shoes? If you have, turn to **153**, but if not, turn to **49**.

8

No, there was no reason for Theo to even have a cross word with Marta, never mind kill her!
Add 15 PURGATORY points, then turn to **150**.

9

This office is quite a big space, yet only Marta and Jan share it. You suppose that's why they put the photocopier in there. You must have been staring at the machine because a voice suddenly asks, 'Do you want to photocopy your bum?'

For a second, you wonder if Marta can see you, but why would she ask you that? And then, a ghost materialises, grinning manically and pointing at the machine. You take in the cloud of white powder over his upper lip and nostrils and shake your head. The last thing you want is to do office pranks with this hyperactive spectre!

'I've done it. Their prints come out with a faint bum print on it.' He starts laughing, bordering on the hysterical, but it's pinged a memory for you. Louisa marching down the corridor, shouting, 'They said they'd fixed this, but it's just the same — this weird fuzzy overlay!' Now you know what it was…

'I presume you had an overdose,' you ask, gesturing to the powder. He looks confused, goes cross-eyed as he tries to see his nose, then laughs again.

'No, I got punched. We were arguing about Sega and Nintendo, and he punched me. I fell, hit my head, and that was it.'

'And which were you arguing for? Sega or Nintendo?'

He looks sheepish at this question.

'Can't remember. Seems a bit silly now because everyone got really into the PlayStation, so it didn't even matter.'

You have to agree — that was a ridiculous reason to die — and record that you have met **CHARLIE**. But then the machine starts whirring and Marta walks over to pluck the printed sheet of paper from it. You glance over and see the word 'Reference' but not who it is for. Marta smirks, pleased with herself, and murmurs, 'If that doesn't get you the job, nothing will. Now, I suppose I should do some actual work.' Tick **CLUE 3**.

She doesn't appear to be pleased with that prospect, so wanders off to the kitchen to grab a Tupperware container from the fridge. Time has flown and, apparently, it's lunchtime. Turn to **220**.

10

The days pass by, fellow ghosts come and go, and at one point you hear that Amsterdam has been completely flooded thanks to rising sea levels! But you've only been dead a month or so, haven't you? Time is, indeed, a bit strange here, so maybe you should go back a little to see if you can do better than the last attempt. You can keep the already acquired clues, codewords, objects and ghosts; just **add 20 PURGATORY** points and turn to **141**.

11

You frown, then ignore Charlie. Marta and Jan's conversation is much more interesting…

'So, when do you start?'

'They want me to do the onboarding at the beginning of next month.'

'Wow, that's not long for Louisa to find your replacement. She's going to be furious!'

'Serves her right. She could've altered my notice period after the probation time, but she didn't. She wanted to be able to get rid of me as quick as possible; well, that works both ways!'

'And so soon after the interviews for Ashley's old position — sucks to be the boss!'
And they both laugh, cackling with Schadenfreude!

'Talking of Ashley,' Marta says, 'She would have been pleased for you. I told you that she knew about your job search, but she never grassed us up to Louisa.'

'Because she wanted me out of here! It was not thanks to the good of her heart!'

'Whatever! Anyway, all's well that ends well.'
And with that, they wander over to the Conference Room — the 'fireside chat' is about to start!
Turn to **104**.

12

Adam is definitely an irritant, but Louisa had absolutely no reason to do him any harm.
Add 15 PURGATORY points, then turn to **150**.

13

But as you waft gently along the landing, Chain-Smoking Ghost appears in a puff of nicotine-stained vapour.

'Oy, you. I've remembered something that might be useful. Or it could be for that stupid dancing drunk girl, I'm not sure.'

You wait expectantly, but when the silence and his perplexed expression continues, you prompt him with a 'Yes? What did you remember?'

He looks affronted and snaps, 'Quid pro quo! What will you give me in return?' You roll your eyes and contemplate floating away, but if you've got something he might appreciate, then why not? Something like… oh, how about cigarettes?

If you found any spectral cigarettes, then turn to **183**, but if not, turn to **200**.

14

She continues humming, then suddenly bellows, 'You're my world, you are my night and day.' It's flat and out of tune, but apparently, this is the chorus. Fortunately, Adam is oblivious to this cacophony; you only wish you were…

'You're my world, you're every breath I take. IF MY LOVE CEASES TO BE— Oh, I've just remembered!'

Seeing as Beehive Ghost had been winding up to a rousing crescendo, you are very relieved that her sudden recall interrupted it.

'There was something that happened one day. Something between you and this Adam, I think.' You ask if she could be any less vague, but your sarcasm is wasted. Beehive Ghost disappears, leaving only fragments of a song behind.

If you have ticked the codeword LIMBO, you can attempt to discover what the ghost was talking about (turn to **78**). If not, you should carry on with your investigation into the motive for your murder.

So, who's next?

| Marta | Turn to **211** |
| Hannah | Turn to **72** |

But if you've already done that, then you should drift towards the landing to think about your strategy (turn to **63**).

15

You follow Adam back to the office, sidestepping as Theo almost barges right through you, then sits down, putting on headphones and disappearing quickly in the code he's writing. Robert hasn't returned yet — maybe he's making a coffee… — and Adam starts to arrange the out-of-office notification.

I will be out of reach this afternoon (10–14) attending the funeral of a dear friend but leave a message and I'll get back to you as soon as I can.

A dear friend? You float through the desk and monitor until you're facing him and study his face. Surely, a 'dear friend' would ping some memories but… no; there's nothing!

It looks like he's preparing to leave soon, so you better be ready to go with him. Except you've watched enough films to know that ghosts can't escape from their place of haunting. Unless, that is, you've learnt a trick from Clara the maid…

If you haven't yet met the ghost called Clara, then you are going to have to abandon any thoughts of attending your own funeral and must turn to **233**.

But if you have, then turn to **Appendix A** (What's on the Desk?) at the back of the book and choose the item that is the solution to Clara's riddle. When you have made your selection and noted its associated number, **return here**.

You must now **ADD the number** to this section, then turn to the new section. If it begins with "It was the logical choice…", then you have chosen correctly, but if not, accept defeat and turn to **233**.

16

There is absolutely no reason why Marta would want Hannah dead — no professional or personal rivalry simmered between them.

 Add 15 PURGATORY points, then turn to **150**.

17

Why else would Hannah have been so angry with you? And it was justified too. She did know about the dastardly promotion sabotage, although ***how*** is anyone's guess!

While you're taking all this in, you float out of the office and can now check out Marta (turn to **217**), but if you've already done that, then turn to **13**.

18

'Marta! Good morning to you. Good weekend?'

'Hi Theo. Is the coffee on?'

You watch as the woman in cycling gear and the man exchange pleasantries, but you soon become bored and drift away. Before you know it, they've left the kitchen and headed off in separate directions. You really must keep a grip on things if you're going to find out what happened to you! Turn to **64**.

19

But your plan is instantly thwarted by the closed door — you can't go through it!

However, if you have ticked the codeword ECTOPLASM, turn to **130**. If not, then you can't enter the server room, and unfortunately, the storeroom door is also closed and therefore, out of bounds. You slump dejectedly and bored onto one of the so-called comfy chairs. Turn to **40**.

20

Even though your computer has already been cleaned and rebooted for the next unfortunate schmuck who works here, the memory is so vivid, it's like you're back at your desk. You can even feel the sticky TAB key…

But despite opening the Office apps and expecting some miraculous revelation to happen, nothing really does.

But the next thing you know is you've created a long document full of flow charts and instructions about haunting — do you think you're going to be onboarding future phantoms? — and now it is the middle of the night and the office is empty.

The hallucination of your laptop has gone too, so you are left contemplating your next move.

If you've ticked the codeword TELEPORTATION, turn to **259** and if not, turn to **13**.

21

However, the ghosts are a bit finicky. If you've already met them, then they will respond. If not, you hang about the offices, shouting, 'Is there anybody there?' but no spectre can be bothered to materialise on command! So, which ghosts have you **already met**?

NSFW Ghost	Turn to **243**
Beehive Ghost	Turn to **175**
Charlie	Turn to **108**
Party Ghost	Turn to **208**

22

After only a few seconds, though, a large, white cat appears. It is sitting nonchalantly on the unit, blinking slowly and occasionally raising a paw to wipe the small trickle of blood that oozes from its nose. That, and the black smudge on its forehead, tells you it was probably hit by a car, although that doesn't really explain why it's here of all places! You give the ghost cat a stroke, then watch as it stretches out its front paw and taps one of the objets d'art. Tap, tap, nudge, nudge, until it topples off onto the carpet. The entire group gasps and stares, before Marta gives a nervous giggle.

'The Marylebone poltergeist strikes again! Or maybe it was Ashley…'

Good grief, have you become a joke already? At least, most of the others have the decency to look mortified by her black humour, but you're sure that Hannah is suppressing a smirk, while Adam simply looks horror-struck! Once Louisa has replaced the ornament, the meeting continues. Turn to **209**.

23

Presumably, it was a nice service but seeing as you fell asleep (or whatever it is that ghosts do), you missed it and only come around when Louisa is leaving and saying a few words to your relatives.

'Such a hard worker and a good team player. I'm sure she would've gone far with her promotion. It was clear early on that she was just right for the Marketing Lead position.'

Louisa delivers all this with a sombre expression — clearly going for the professional look — but that changes when your mother says, 'Oh yes, Ashley told us all about you.'

A simple sentence, but you can feel a shockwave of panic and paranoia rush through Louisa, before she gives them a grimace-like smile and moves away. Tick **CLUE 6**.

However much you'd like to stay and try to find out what's behind it all and what you'd apparently told your family, you are linked to Louisa and when she goes to the car park, you go too. It's an awkward meeting between her, Jan and Adam — they can hardly ignore each other! — but while Louisa is explaining that she'd love to give them a lift back to the office but she has an errand to run first, you spot a strange woman who is staring in your direction. You look around to see what's caught her eye and notice a group of battered, tattered musicians. Maybe you've got enough time to go and investigate one of these oddities, but who? The strange woman (turn to **160**) or the musicians (turn to **273**)?

24

With just the thought of following him, you move effortlessly out of the office, along the corridor and into the kitchen. Which is somewhat disappointing, as you assumed you would pass through the walls… The man — tall and well dressed, with short, dark hair and an easy charm — is dancing while simultaneously singing and pouring water into the coffee machine.

"In the code that Adam wrote,
Are mistakes that will not run,
And he boasts about his brain
But his work is never done

Adam's not a better programmer than me, programmer than me, programmer than me…"

Tick **CLUE 5**. As he continues, you realise that it's a **Beatles song** — oh, what's the name? Your mind is so foggy! — and feel sorry for Adam. It's a bit cruel and big-headed of this man, and you wonder if he ever sang nasty songs about you…

'For God's sake, Theo, I was on the phone! At least tell me that you've been useful and put the coffee on!'

He smiles, swallows a piece of chocolate and shouts, 'Of course, I have, Hannah. And I know you love my songs, you little tease.'

There's no answer from Hannah, but you're more interested in exploring your new role as office ghost. What kind of haunting can you actually do? If you want to try to move an object, turn to **136**, but if you'd rather make a spine-tingling groan, turn to **98**.

25

Marta is obviously an office thief — you don't need to be a detective to know that! — but was she worried that you knew about her criminal secret? It could be a motive; however, she used the present tense in the statement "you-know-who *hasn't* said anything"? Seeing as you're dead, you can't be 'you-know-who'!

And that means, Marta would have no reason to murder you. This is progress, indeed, but it would be good to know who the mystery person is too. If you have ticked CLUE 11, turn to **234**, but remember **this section number** because you will have to return here afterwards!

Although you're deep in thought, you got enough wits left to notice the packet of cigarettes on the shelf opposite. That's unusual, so you give it a poke and to your amazement, your finger doesn't go straight through — the packet moves! That's got to be useful, so you grab the **spectral cigarettes**, wait for the ectoplasm to build up again, then leave.

Marta is back at her desk, so you can now check out Adam (turn to **278**) or Hannah (turn to **72**).

But if you've already done that, then drift towards the landing to think about your strategy (turn to **63**).

26

You wander up and down, sidling between the bikes, until you see something unusual on the floor. It's a 7-inch vinyl record — Cilla Black, to be precise, singing "You're My World" — and it's incongruous enough to make you stop and examine it further. When you realise that you can actually pick it up, you know that it is a ghostly object. Make a note that you have found a **spectral vinyl record**, but there is nothing else other than the exit to the service tunnel and that is closed. However, if you have ticked the codeword ECTOPLASM and wish to open the door, turn to **238**. If not, then you feel a strange compulsion to return to your own office — is something calling you? — but do you want to go via the normal stairs (turn to **260**) or the creepy, not-often-used back staircase (turn to **77**)?

27

'You have to be joking!'

Hannah seems to think that this is sarcasm, so after giving a withering stare, she walks away.

Although you're quite happy to continue with the bingo, too many people are moving around this small space, making both time and the surroundings shift and judder. By the time everything settles again, Louisa is announcing the next activity. Turn to **275**.

28

However, he has closed the door, but surely that is no problem for you. Thinking that self-belief is all that's needed, you stride confidently towards the door but then — 'Argh! Damn it!' — and you are suddenly sprawled on the floorboards, clutching your nose.

'How can a ghost not walk through a door?' The question is delivered to thin air, so it's a shock when someone actually answers. You leap to your feet and turn to the window. A woman is leaning nonchalantly against the frame and she looks ready to party, albeit in the nineties. Does she work here?

'You can hear me? Are you dead too?'

The woman laughs.

'Of course, I am! It was the Christmas party 1990 and I was drunk. I needed some fresh air so I decided to lean out of the window…' She gestures to the outside with her hand and in that moment, you see that the right side of her skull is staved in.

She shrugs and says philosophically, 'Daft, but at least it was quick. Anyhow, as I was saying, it's not an automatic right for us to walk through walls or doors. There is a way, but I've forgotten. That's another consequence of my stupid death — I'm always drunk!'

Make a note that you have met **PARTY GHOST**.

But before you can ask her anything else, she disappears, so you look around. At this end of the short corridor, there are the toilets but you can't get inside. However, at that moment, the office door opens and the man reappears. He heads to the kitchen, but you hear a woman shouting from the room he's just left.

'Jan, you should try out Naan Nirvana. They did the most gorgeous lamb vindaloo I've ever eaten!'

You watch as he smiles, then says, 'And you've eaten a lot, Marta!'

She laughs and while he searches through the fridge, you feel a memory tugging at your mind. She called him 'Jan' — pronounced Yan — it sounds European and that's ringing a bell! But before you can have an epiphany, he swears and shouts, 'Who's taken my spring roll? As if I don't know!' His dramatic exit happens to be straight through you, and once the mad swirling has settled, you are alone in the small corridor.

You head back to the landing and could either go left (turn to **230**), right (turn to **32**) or venture down the stairs (turn to **177**).

29

Theo is strutting around like a peacock, joking and chatting.

'I suppose you heard of the death here. Very sad, she'd just got the promotion to Marketing Lead. Mind you, that was contentious. Hannah, who has the job now, was up for it too but didn't get it. Said she'd been sabotaged but was that sour grapes?' Tick **CLUE 1**.

With his flippant and disrespectful attitude, you feel a surge of anger and look around for an outlet.

Ah-ha, the networked screen on the adjacent wall. Now, that's a thought, but this will only work if you have ticked the codeword OUIJA. If you have, turn to **258**, but if you haven't, turn to **135**.

30

It's not like the shoes came with any instructions, so you're not sure what to expect. However, they fit you perfectly — presumably, phantom shoes fit everyone's feet — and then you wait until Robert is alone. The clock ticks past 5 PM, Theo leaves first, then Adam, with an obvious sense of superiority, gets his coat on. Once the door closes, you start to parade up and down the office.

The effect is instant. Robert gasps and looks around wide-eyed, hoping for a rational explanation, but the clacking of your heels continues up and down the floorboards. With all this energy, you weirdly start to manifest a smell too. The aroma of Thai curry fills the air and Robert puts two and two together.

'Ashley, is that you?' He wails. 'I'm sorry what happened to you, but it wasn't me. I swear it wasn't me. I heard who gave you the curry though. It was Hannah. Not me. It was Hannah!' He's becoming hysterical now, but it sounds like the truth. Hannah gave you the poisoned curry!

If you have been given a gold ribbon, turn to **266**, but if not, turn to **75**.

31

It's not that the start-up failed; it's that Theo had been stealing IP! That's what he's worried about and with good reason — counterfeit fraud could land him in prison!

Did Theo think that you knew something about his start-up crimes? And if so, would it be a reason to murder you?

Despite having no answers for that, you have discovered the **TRUTH about Theo** and decide to continue while you're on a roll. Turn to **213**.

32

Through the only door, you find yourself in a spacious office. There are skylights in the vaulted ceiling and three desks. The man you saw before is already at his desk, giving the impression of being hard at work, but when you glide around to view his screen, you see that he's scrolling through a clothes website. As you drift to the other desks, you spot a **banana** on the floor. You don't remember seeing that when you came in, but surely there's no such thing as a ghost banana…

There is, however, a ghost woman standing in front of a cupboard.

'I think the banana is for you,' she says, before coughing loud and long. You estimate she's from the Sixties. The beehive hairdo is a dead giveaway, plus the brown miniskirt and thickly lined eyes, but her face is congested and purple.

'Bloody chocolate! Took just one at a retirement party, then that randy sod, Roger Blenkins, tried to cop a feel and the next thing you know, I choked to death. I didn't even manage to slap him. Just gasped and inhaled the bloody thing. A Walnut Whip, can you believe it!'

You feel it only right to commiserate for such a pointless death but then ask her why the banana is for you — it's not like you can eat it. However, she simply shrugs, clueless too.

'Well, it's not for me, so it must be for you. I don't think it's his,' and she points at the man, who is now taking a selfie for some inexplicable reason.

'Although he is a peacock! And watch out for the others in here. One isn't above having a bit of hanky panky himself at work and the other is a bit of a liar who's always making out that he's better than he really is.'

'And me? Do you remember me?'

She looks across, tilting the beehive alarmingly to the side as she scrutinises you.

'You were in the other office. You had a cold. Surely you didn't die of a cold, did you?'

At that crucial moment, the door swings wide open and two men enter, one striding through Beehive Ghost and the other stepping squarely on the banana, and both woman and fruit disappear. Record that you have met **BEEHIVE GHOST**.

The atmosphere seems to instantly tighten, and despite the polite nods and mentioning of each other's names 'Theo…Adam…Robert,' it is clear that there is no love lost between these three men. And what's worse, you still don't recognise anyone! This is very frustrating, but as quickly as they arrive, all three exit the office. Apparently, there's a meeting, so you decide to follow them. Turn to **225**.

33

You drift into the vaulted office and see Adam sitting there. Interesting but not entirely surprising that Clara thinks he's weaselly…

He is typing furiously like a concert pianist and gives the impression that he's some master programmer, but when you peer at the screen, see that he's accessed Facebook and is writing a long post about how much he misses his good friend. '…Taken too soon.' Once he's inserted the sad face emoji, he sits back, waiting. For what? Sympathy?

Whatever it is, it doesn't come fast enough for Adam's liking, so he starts typing again. 'Possible soulmate but we'll never know now…' Urgh, did Adam have a crush on you? And if so, does that make him more or less likely to murder you?

The cleaner appears in the doorway with a clatter as her mop bucket hits the door frame. Adam jumps, then blushes as if he's been caught doing something wrong, which, to be honest, he was. Claiming these hours as overtime is a bit cheeky…

'Whoops-a-daisy, pet. Sorry to disturb you.'
Adam mumbles something as he starts to pack his stuff away, but you couldn't hear it and the cleaner isn't paying any attention. Do you want to visit the boss woman now? If you do, turn to **269**; however, if you've already spied on her, then your next move depends on whether you've ticked the codeword TELEPORTATION. If you have ticked it, turn to **259** and if not, turn to **13**.

34

So, Hannah's suspicions, accusations and fury with you were justified — she *did* know about the dastardly promotion sabotage, although how is anyone's guess!

While you're taking all this in, you float out of the office and can now check out Marta (turn to **211**) or Adam (turn to **278**), but if you've already done that, then turn to **63**.

35

There's a slightly unpleasant smell of reheated bacon lingering in the kitchen, and when you stick your head into the refrigerator, see that there is only one green-lidded Tupperware left. Maybe that's all there was, or maybe everyone zoomed in here at 12 to grab their lunch.

But at that moment, you hear clickety heels marching purposefully and Hannah appears, phone in hand. It starts to ring as she's reaching for the green Tupperware, but this is not a problem for Ms Professional here! Ever the multitasker, she's answering the call, while pouring a coffee and grabbing a fork. She then sweeps back to her office in a cloud of self-imposed importance. Which is almost as unpalatable as the bacon…

Tick the codeword **MEANS** and think about the next stage of your investigation. If you've ticked the codeword OPPORTUNITY, turn to **246**, if not, turn to **6**.

36

Sounding like a balloon popping, the spectral fart echoes around the office, and Adam purposefully marches to the door and snatches up the mail. You glide after him, down the steep stairs, around the corner and into the offices below. The layout is similar but with a brand colour scheme of chocolate brown and teal, and promotional posters of happy, smiling people. It's really not clear what their business is — something to do with dentistry, perhaps? — but then again, you still don't remember what your own company does!

Adam drops the mail wordlessly on a nearby table, looks confused, then turns to leave, but just then, a man pops his head out of the adjacent office.

'Oh, it's you. It's been a while, Adam. I've been looking out for you. Hang on a minute.'

He disappears into their kitchen, and while Adam waits politely in the lounge area, you follow — any excuse for a nosy around! They have a much better coffee machine than you do, but the more shocking thing is what he has retrieved from the back of a cupboard.

'Here you go. You must've thought I'd nicked it! But thanks for lending it.' And with that, he hands over a burgundy Tupperware bowl. Adam looks flustered, then grabs it and rushes out of the office. Hmm, that could be useful information, but you've also noticed something else. A slightly ajar door…

It's probably nothing, but while you're here, you might as well check it out. Turn to **206**.

37

Hannah is sitting at her desk, typing emails, sending meeting invites and inputting data into a spreadsheet. Was this *your* job? Did you actually enjoy this? Who knows?

Still, Hannah does seem to care about her position, so perhaps she was jealous when you got the promotion. Is that enough of a reason for her to kill you, though?

If you found CLUE 4 AND you have ticked the codeword MIASMA, there is something you should definitely investigate first — turn to **292**.

If not, then maybe you've recently discovered an interesting skill and want to try it now — if you've ticked the codeword LIMBO, turn to **163**.

If you have neither of these options, then you give up on Hannah and can now check out Marta (turn to **217**).

And if you've already done that, turn to **13**.

38

You are well aware, then, of the professional rivalry between Adam and Theo. Both men thought they were the alpha at work, only Theo was the actual Team Lead, and that was a source of intense jealousy for Adam. Remember, how he kept trying to promote himself. Yes, he wanted Theo gone so he could take his rightful place. But what was Adam's plan? If you have ticked CLUE 10, turn to **102**. If not, turn to **50**.

39

Ah, yes, there really was no love lost between these two, but would Theo have killed Adam simply for being annoying? They also shared an office, so maybe Theo was worried that Adam had discovered his illegal goings-on. However, Adam never mentioned that — he just went on and on about the presentation! In fact, when you really think about it, Theo had no motive for murdering Adam.
Add 5 PURGATORY points, then turn to **150**.

40

However, after only five minutes of boredom, a figure strides into this communal area and heads to the storeroom — here's your chance! You slide through the gap and watch as Marta rummages through the neatly stocked items. She grabs some pens, but to your shock, she then takes a toner cartridge and secretes it under her cardigan. She's a sneaky thief! Tick **CLUE 2**. And with her ill-gotten gains, she leaves. You'd like to stay and have a root around, but being trapped with only paperclips for company is not how you'd like to spend eternity! Before the door shuts, you exit too. Turn to **277**.

41

Suddenly, you are enveloped in a fragrant mist. The aroma of lemongrass, coconut milk and coriander fills your nostrils, and once you've taken a deep sniff — that smells delicious! — you open your eyes to see a bowl of Thai curry in a burgundy Tupperware bowl on the table.

And not just a bowl, but *the* bowl! Memories once more flood your brain. It's the bowl of Thai curry that you ate on your last day in the office. The poisoned curry, filled with bamboo shoots, red peppers and paracetamol!

But you never brought leftovers into the office. If you didn't go out to get lunch, then you brought a sandwich in. Never meals! And the Tupperware tells you that it was definitely from someone's home.

'Oh, such malice aforethought!' you state dramatically and Conscripted Ghost smiles, appreciating either your literary language or the progress you're making in solving your own murder, but there's no denying the harsh facts.

Someone in this office made a Thai curry, laced it, brought it to the office and enticed you to eat it. But who and why? What have you done to deserve this?

'Onwards and upwards, new ghost. After all, you've not really got anything else to do.'

Conscripted Ghost makes a good point, so that's what you do. Turn to **250**.

42

The cacophony gets louder as you draw closer — the walls are vibrating! — but no one else reacts. It is something supernatural! Through the slightly ajar door to the server room, smoke pours and the air shimmers with heat, but still, you figure that it can't actually kill you, so in you go.

Piled on the floor is a heap of ash with an abandoned foot sticking out of it. You stare, gaping, then realise that a charred, vaguely human-shaped ghost is also staring at it. The smell of crispy bacon is almost overwhelming, but you manage to ask, 'Is that you?' It scoffs, then says, 'Yes. I died well before that, though, thank goodness. It was after the Blitz and I had nowhere to stay, so I broke in here for a place to kip. I might have had a bit to drink too. A cigarette and a couple of hours later and that was that…'

How sozzled do you have to be to sleep through being burnt to death!? Still, although his combustion wasn't exactly spontaneous, he didn't actually suffer.

'And then they put in all this new-fangled stuff. I don't understand it, but when I put my hands on this wire—' and he demonstrates with his charred sausage-like fingers, '—you can send magic messages!'

It looks like the ghost you've just nicknamed 'Frazzles' is grabbing the WLAN cable, so maybe the magic messages are emails or chat messages. Seriously? Can you communicate with the Living this way? This is a major advantage to any phantom in your situation, so tick the codeword **OUIJA**.

Suddenly, an idea pops into your head — this would be a useful way to request attendance information and perhaps identify who had the opportunity for murder! You decide to strike while the iron is hot and before you inexplicably vanish or find that a year has passed, but don't worry, you can continue the MEANS investigation afterwards. Turn to **85**.

43

'Is that a horse?'

You jolt, shocked, and realise that time has marched on. Hannah is currently staring out of the window at the animal trotting up and down the concourse. You drift over and concur that it is, indeed, a phantom horse. Hannah snorts in disgust, then floats towards the lounge area. On the way, Party Ghost materialises by the kitchen, dancing and laughing, but when she spots Hannah, shouts, 'Hey, Plant Pot Ghost. How's it going?'

However, Hannah is in no mood for friendly conversation and simply ignores her.

'Don't worry. After a few decades, she'll forgive you. It was an accident, after all!' You smile at Party Ghost, grateful that she's taking your side, but not convinced that Hannah will ever forgive you! In the lounge, though, there are bigger fish to fry, as today is not a normal office day — it's a Head Office Visit day! This should be interesting…

Meredith (CEO), Justin (CFO) and Kelsey (COO), plus their minions, are here, and they wanted to have individual meet-and-greets and a 'fireside chat', but the recent events have eclipsed those plans.

'One death would be bad enough,' yells Meredith, clearly audible through the glass walls of Louisa's office, 'But two! In a month! Do you have any idea what this could do to our reputation?'

All the Living look shell-shocked; presumably, Hannah's dramatic death has taken its toll on them, although there is still a frisson of excitement with the ongoing argument. Sensing that this needs to be curtailed, Justin starts to herd everyone into the Conference Room, before urgently whispering to his assistant, 'Where's Kelsey?'

Seconds later, that mystery is solved, as she reappears. But she is deathly-white and mumbling, 'I saw them. I know I saw them. Rushing into the subway. A crowd of mutants. I swear, they were not human. Mutants!'

Justin rolls his eyes — could this day get any worse? — and instructs another assistant to deal with the psychotic COO, then he claps his hands and announces that the fireside chat will start soon.

Turn to **294**.

44

'Of course, I've still got the big bar I found yesterday. It isn't going to eat itself, you know!' Jan smiles and whispers, 'When does this waste of time finish?' Theo just nods and smiles even more, before clapping him on the back, walking away.

You then realise that Jan has written the number "**7**" on his card, which is weird, and although you're quite happy to continue with the bingo, too many people are moving around this small space, making both time and the surroundings shift and judder. By the time everything settles again, Louisa is announcing the next activity. Turn to **275**.

45

How many PURGATORY points do you have?

20 or less Turn to **201**
25 or more Turn to **188**

46

Robert did spill the beans about Adam's so-called doctor's appointment, which was actually time spent skiving off work, but he didn't learn that until much later. No, there was no reason for Adam to even think about murdering Robert.

Add 10 PURGATORY points, then turn to **195**.

47

There is a moment of trepidation as you approach the coffin, but you ignore it, stick your head in through the side and come face-to-face with yourself! Immediately, it is clear that there was no fancy embalming done — just a wash and hair comb — and through the fabric of the dress, you see the thick black sutures from the post-mortem and bruises and puncture sites on your arms.

Hmm, evidence of IV drips, which means you were in hospital, but what with? There's thick make-up on your face, but even that can't disguise your waxy complexion. Well, you are a corpse, so what did you expect? But what's more surprising is the packet of cigarettes tucked down the side of the coffin. You're 99% sure that you didn't smoke, so why are they here? With that thought, you give a cautious prod and realise that you can actually pick them up. They are **spectral cigarettes**! This is odd, so you decide to keep them, then hear a loud, projected voice. The service has started, so you glide over to the mourners. Who are you tethered to for this escape?

Adam	Turn to **103**
Jan	Turn to **261**
Louisa	Turn to **23**

48

So, Louisa was dismissed for racial discrimination and she plainly hasn't changed her ways! She was always having a go at Jan, simply because he was Polish. You watch as Louisa scrutinises the 'likes' and sees your tiny profile photo. She doesn't say anything, just harrumphs.

Naturally, you can't remember how or why you knew Astrid Pomeroy, but it's safe to say that you weren't Louisa's biggest fan…

Is this her motive? Did you know she was racist? Was she worried that you'd reveal her dismissal from another job over it? That probably would be a good reason to get rid of you, but wouldn't it have been easier to just sack you? Less police involvement, surely!

You have discovered the **TRUTH about Louisa**.

You feel a bit sick — finding tangible evidence that someone might have murdered you is enough to upset anyone's stomach — but Louisa is finished now.

'You look a bit green. Under all that yellow, I mean.'

You shriek and spin around to face NSFW Ghost, who has materialised behind you. If you haven't done so yet, record that you have met **NSFW GHOST**. He's so close he could touch and in fact…

'Keep your distance, you pervert!'

He gives a good-natured grin, then shrugs as he withdraws his groping hand.

'Well, if I had something that entertained me, I wouldn't have to sneak up on you, would I?'

You're tempted to lecture him about harassment in the workplace, then wonder whether you do have something. If you have found a spectral newspaper and want to give it to him, turn to **285**, but if you don't have one or don't feel so generous, you could visit the weaselly man now (turn to **216**).

However, if you've already spied on him, then your next move depends on whether you've ticked the codeword TELEPORTATION. If you have ticked it, turn to **259** and if not, turn to **13**.

49

Your investigation has been good so far, but without any way to make the guilty party confess, you have reached a dead end (pardon the pun…)

And so, the strange laws of physics that govern purgatory unleash a sickening swirling of the air and a piercing screech as time is forced backwards.

You find yourself on the landing talking to a distinctly Seventies-dressed, chain-smoking ghost. He is leering and saying with far-too-much enthusiasm, 'Maybe you were murdered!'

You have been given a second chance. You can keep the already acquired clues, codewords, objects and ghosts; just **add 40 PURGATORY** points, then turn to **1**.

50

Really? You never saw a single occasion in which Theo stole someone else's food from the office fridge? Unbelievable! **Add 5 PURGATORY** points. He did it all the time and would eat it without a flicker of a guilty conscience.

And then Adam could hint that Theo actually meant to take his own life, seeing as his close friend, Danesh, had also died of a paracetamol overdose. Oh, it could have been so neat, so easy. So, what went wrong?

If you have ticked CLUE 7, turn to **60**. If not, turn to **280**.

51

With no way to take your irritation out on Jan, you simply stomp out of the office. Silently, of course…

You can now either check out Hannah (turn to **37**) or Marta (turn to **217**), but if you've already done that, then turn to **13**.

52

Aahh, the classic motive — jilted man murders former lover. The only problem with this theory is that Louisa broke up with Robert *after* your murder. **Add 5 PURGATORY** points, then turn to **150**.

53

You had concentrated so much on trying to get Theo to go towards Hannah, you accidentally let out a tiny fart. If you haven't done so yet, you can now tick the codeword **MIASMA**.

'And? I suppose you're going to make some sarcastic comment about it.' Her arms are crossed — she looks defensive, knowing that this film choice does not fit well with her polished image and wondering why she had told Marta — the most indiscreet person in the office! — in the first place? Theo just smirks, imagining all the teasing he can do now!

You then realise that Theo has written the number "**7**" on his card, which is weird, and although you're quite happy to continue with the bingo, too many people are moving around this small space, making both time and the surroundings shift and judder. The next thing you know is that Louisa is announcing the final activity. Turn to **275**.

54

Without warning, your feet begin to rise as though they're filled with helium! The rest of you flips upside down, and you are unceremoniously dragged higher and higher, through the ceiling and into the attic. At which point, the phenomenon stops and you collapse at the feet of a Grey Lady Ghost. Long grey hair, long grey dress (which could have been from anytime between medieval and Victorian) and grey skin.

'Oh hello, I've never been up here before. Well, of course, I haven't, why would I?'
Stop babbling, you tell yourself, then ask, 'Why are you haunting this place?' Which could be considered a very insensitive question if the poor woman has been murdered here…
Luckily, she just shrugs.

''I'm a generic ghost. People everywhere, in every time, have always seen Grey Lady Ghosts. It's a combination of poor lighting, poor eyesight and alcohol! When one has been imagined so many times, one tends to be brought into existence.'
Well, that's unexpected! And for a few seconds, you are speechless, but eventually ask, 'And did you make me come up here? Why?'

'You have my opera glasses and I'm expected at the Marylebone Theatre soon for a stint of haunting there. Grey Lady Ghosts and theatres are a classic combination.'
That's fair enough, so you hand the glasses over. The Grey Lady turns to leave, then pauses and says, 'You're the latest one, aren't you? I know that you

shouldn't have died. The intended victim was a man. Does that help?'

But without waiting for a reply, she disappears, and you gently sink through the rafters and back into the office. Turn to **257**.

55

However, the ghosts are a bit finicky. If you've already met them, then they will respond to you. If not, you hang about the offices, shouting, 'Is there anybody there?' but no spectre can be bothered to materialise on command! So, which ghosts have you **already met**?

>   NSFW Ghost   Turn to **243**
>   Beehive Ghost   Turn to **175**
>   Charlie   Turn to **108**
>   Party Ghost   Turn to **208**

56

It's only the fact that you're already dead that emboldens you — after all, the likeliest outcomes are being grabbed by some monstrous, aquatic animal or falling in and drowning in stagnant, slimy water! But although the wood creaks under the strain, you squeeze through the railings and reach down, stretching both hands and all your fingers until they dip through the lurid green algae.

Keeping a careful eye on the creature, which has turned and is now swimming in your direction, you reach deeper and deeper and finally touch the hard rubber casing of a torch. There is a sudden commotion in the water as the creature darts forward. Something smooth, soft and cold completely envelops you — like a thick jelly glove! — but with lightning-fast reflexes, your hand, still grasping the submerged light, retracts instantly.

Make a note that you have found a **torch**! On the downside, though, however many times you try to wipe your hands, they stay green. Which is unfortunate…

Tick the codeword **CAUL**.

Oh well, you can deal with that later. It's time to get away from this smelly moat and the weird creature, so you head through the gap. Turn to **187**.

57

And with a sinking sensation in the pit of your stomach, the pieces fall into place. Hannah's private message to you in which she let off steam about Louisa. The message that you made sure Louisa read and included the phrase "can't organise a **** in a brewery!"

This congratulations email with its odd mention of a brewery was Louisa's way of letting Hannah know that she knew.

You sigh. Hannah knew exactly what you'd done. You have discovered the **TRUTH about Hannah**. She must have been beyond angry with your betrayal, but did she actually kill you?

You still don't know that — Hannah might have motive, but you need more evidence to know for sure — but on the positive side, at least your hands are no longer green. **Strike off** the codeword CAUL. After another sigh, you decide to continue what you were doing, but were you going to the boss woman (turn to **178**) or the weaselly man (turn to **33**)?

58

Charlie calls you over, bouncing like a hyperactive toddler and hissing, 'They're celebrating. They're celebrating! Do you think they'll have any blow?'

Before you answer that, you should turn to **170** if you have discovered the TRUTH about Jan. If not, turn to **106**.

59

You're absolutely convinced that you know where the prize is and glide through the office until reaching the server room. However, Robert and Adam must have gone somewhere else! Seconds later, you hear a triumphant shout and realise that they found the prize and you didn't!

There's no time to be peeved about it though, as Louisa is wrapping up the team bonding session. And not a moment too soon. She looks like she's going to spend her lunch break in the nearest wine bar! Everyone heads either to their desks or the toilet, and you end up floating aimlessly in the large, vaulted office. Turn to **214**.

60

The Thai curry was made with coconut milk, and you know that there were many occasions when Theo refused to consume coconut — the pina colada, the Bounty bars, and the Tom Kha Gai — and that's just for starters! He had a serious allergy to coconut. In fact, a whiff of coconut would send him into an anaphylactic shock. Theo may have thought about stealing the Thai curry in the burgundy Tupperware, but one look would have made him abandon that idea instantly! Which is why it remained in the fridge until Hannah saw it and thought, 'This must be Louisa's lunch. How's about this for a good way to get revenge for the promotion sabotage.' Turn to **70**.

61

Ah, yes, Adam. He didn't really seem to have any friends, did he? Definitely a bit of a weird loner, but you think he is also a murderer?

Well, it was eventually revealed that he did have burgundy Tupperware, and he was a very frequent customer at the local Thai restaurant…

You are right — **subtract 20 PURGATORY** points — Adam did buy the takeaway curry, transferred it into his own Tupperware, added copious amounts of paracetamol, then stashed it in the fridge. But why? Why would he do that? Who was his intended victim?

You	Turn to **114**
Hannah	Turn to **276**
Jan	Turn to **179**
Robert	Turn to **46**
Louisa	Turn to **146**
Theo	Turn to **210**
Marta	Turn to **263**

62

Well, that would show him, wouldn't it? These foreigners coming over here and taking all our jobs — how dare they? They need taking down a peg or two! Is that what Louisa did? Or maybe it was because he'd made complaints about her. These are all good ideas, but Jan said that the complaints were ignored and nothing changed. Therefore, Louisa had no reason to kill Jan because she could carry on her odious behaviour with impunity.

Add 5 PURGATORY points, then turn to **150**.

63

After all this, the interviews are over and everyone is working, pretending to work or simply killing time before they can go home. This is good news for you, as you can continue your sleuthing, but inexplicably, you fall asleep. The hours pass until you realise that you are in a cloud of cigarette smoke and someone is prodding you.

It's Chain-Smoking Ghost!

'Are you ill? You've been very still for a very long time.'

You can see the station clock through the window and realise that it's evening — you've wasted a whole afternoon of investigating!

Feeling that you'd like to get something else out of this day, you ask if anyone is still in the office and to your surprise, he nods.

'Yes, the boss woman and the weaselly man.' That's dedication! So, who would you like to visit?

> Boss woman   Turn to **178**
> Weaselly man   Turn to **33**

64

But before you can even think about what to do next, there is a clatter of more footsteps coming up the stairs. You peer over the landing to see who else works here. Will any of them reveal how you died? Turn to **248**.

65

At first you grab the HDMI cable, making the monitor display resize, rotate, then flick on and off! Eventually, though, you manage to send a message to Robert's inbox.

`This is Ashley. I know you heard who gave me the poisoned food. I am here. Just say the name out loud.`

However, the monitor mishaps make Robert think it is IT tomfoolery rather than the ghost of his co-worker trying to make contact.

'I am sick and tired of you two idiots! Enough with the childish hacking nonsense!'

Adam and Theo both jolt up, look at each other, then back to Robert before yelling.

'If something's happened, it's that moron. You know what he's like!'

'Desperate for attention, that's him. He lies and makes stuff up — you know that!' And then Adam stalks out of the room, hissing, 'I've had enough!' as he goes, heading towards Louisa's office. Next, Theo storms out too. Robert seems stunned by this development and simply stares at your message on the screen, apparently unsure about what to do next.

Should you follow Adam (turn to **118**) or Theo (turn to **291**) or stay with Robert (turn to **7**)?

66

She smiles and waves when she sees you, then nods towards Adam, saying, 'Did you hear that? Blimey, I bet that Theo's ears burn with what this one says about him. He's always stirring up trouble. Telling tales and trying to drop him in it. The thing is, though, it's usually this one that makes the mistakes, so he just makes himself look stupid. There is so much rivalry, that's for sure.' Tick **CLUE 5**.

Following that juicy bit of gossip, she starts humming a song as she floats around Adam's desk, and despite it being an old song, there's a chance that you recognise it…

If you managed to find a vinyl record, turn to **262**, but if you haven't, turn to **14**.

67

However, if you've found CLUE 3, you must turn immediately to **196**. If not, continue reading…

Following Jan might be a nice idea, but you haunt the offices and, therefore, can't go wandering off willy-nilly. Unless, that is, you know of a way to ESCAPE.
If you do know, you could do that **now**, but if you don't (or, indeed, you'd prefer to stay here), then you are stuck in the office!
Do you want to monitor the interviews (turn to **107**) or simply hang around the remaining workers, hoping to catch them off guard (turn to **242**)?

68

And with that, she exits the storeroom. Although you're in shock, you got enough wits left to notice the packet of cigarettes on the shelf opposite. That's unusual, so you give it a poke and to your amazement, your finger doesn't go straight through — the packet moves! That's got to be useful, so you grab the **spectral cigarettes**, wait for the ectoplasm to build up again, then leave.
Marta is back at her desk, so you can now check out Hannah (turn to **37**), but if you've already done that, then turn to **13**.

69

Adam looks quite disturbed with this assumption and snaps; ''No! That's not me!' then walks away frowning.

Although you're quite happy to continue with the bingo, too many people are moving around this small space, making both time and the surroundings shift and judder. By the time everything settles again, Louisa is announcing the next activity. Turn to **275**.

70

For a while, you are too stunned to do anything. You thought you'd come to terms with the fact that your death was collateral damage in someone else's vendetta, but to realise that it was only ever about Adam's inferiority complex…

What an utterly pointless reason for you to die!

Nevertheless, you have solved your own murder, so you glance around, wondering if the bright vortex will whisk you away to the next realm. But nothing happens. The office remains the same, boring place, and you thump your fists against the nearest desk in frustration. Your temper isn't improved when your hands pass noiselessly through the furniture, but it does give you a spark of inspiration. Of course! Adam must confess. You must have justice if you are ever going to be able to move on. With a crackling energy that makes the lights flicker as you float past, you head to the vaulted office and put the phantom shoes on. Turn to **212**.

71

Glancing at the wall clock, you see that it's almost noon. Lunchtime! No time like the present to check out your fellow office workers' dietary habits.

If you want to canvas the ghosts who haunt the particular offices of your colleagues and benefit from their lengthy observations, turn to **21**. However, if you'd rather hang out in the kitchen to discover what everyone eats, turn to **126**.

72

Hannah is sitting at her desk, typing emails, sending meeting invites and inputting data into a spreadsheet. Was this *your* job? Did you actually enjoy this? Who knows?

Still, Hannah does seem to care about her position, so perhaps she was jealous when you got the promotion. Is that enough of a reason for her to kill you, though?

If you found CLUE 4 AND you have ticked the codeword MIASMA, there is something you should definitely investigate first — turn to **180**.

If not, then maybe you've recently discovered an interesting skill and want to try it now — if you've ticked the codeword LIMBO, turn to **120**.

If you have neither of these options, then you give up on Hannah and can now check out Adam (turn to **278**) or Marta (turn to **211**). And if you've already done that, then drift to the landing to think about your strategy (turn to **63**).

73

Hannah said that she just wanted to get back at you, and you know that she had a very good reason to want revenge. You shared her nasty email ***about*** Louisa ***with*** Louisa which is why Hannah didn't stand a chance of getting the promotion. And what's more, thanks to Louisa's congratulations email, Hannah knew that you'd done it. But would she risk everything to murder you or would getting you in trouble for the petty theft of the Thai curry be enough to satisfy her? You have to answer that question right now.

So, do you believe that Hannah ***did not*** put the paracetamol in the curry (turn to **197**) or do you think that she is guilty and is lying in order to shift the blame off her own shoulders (turn to **299**)?

74

Through the glass of the corner office — Louisa's office — you see a ghost sitting at the desk in front of a shimmering, transparent huge computer monitor, and from the hand movements in his trousers, you're pretty sure he's not doing any work! Suddenly, he sees you watching and smiles, beckoning you over. Despite his inappropriate behaviour, he seems harmless enough, so you go in.

'Oh, come on, don't be so judgemental! We'd only just got the internet. What else was I going to do? Mind you, in my time, this office had proper walls, so you could get away with watching naughty stuff then. That was until I had a heart attack. Very embarrassing. Credit to them, though. They zipped me back up and didn't tell my wife. You're new, aren't you?'

'Yes, and I'm trying to find out how I died and why I'm stuck here. Can you help?'

With an excited sense of purpose, he stands up and glides effortlessly through the desk, then grabs you by the shoulders. You give a quick glance of disgust at his hands — after all, you know where they've been! — then look back at his face. He's got an earnest expression and says, 'Ectoplasm!'

'Excuse me?'

'It took forever for me to learn things here, but the most important thing is that you will definitely need ectoplasm.'

He lets go, then holds out his hand. A small glob of mucus starts to hang down off his fingertip in a perfect teardrop, and you feel slightly queasy. It's not… is it? It can't be! Oh, that's sick! As if he's read your mind, he snaps, 'No, it's not THAT. It's ectoplasm. Just hold a digit out and it'll start to pool up then drip off. And the key thing is, any door handle you drop it on will open. It's the only way to get through closed doors, seeing as we can't actually walk through walls! Good, eh?'

Well, it's better than nothing, so tick the codeword **ECTOPLASM**, but if you're hoping that he has other useful tips, you'd be wrong. Instead, he abruptly vanishes when the others return from your funeral. Record that you have met **NSFW GHOST**. Unfortunately, other than a few comments like, 'It was a nice service,' nothing much is said! Everyone starts to head back to their desks, so you must decide how to fill the rest of the afternoon. Turn to **115**.

75

Feeling overwhelmed, you stop walking and take the shoes off. In the sudden silence, Robert wipes the tears from his cheeks, now embarrassed with his performance, but as he exits the office, he mutters, 'It *was* Hannah.'

You wait, wondering if this breakthrough is what's needed to catapult you into a better afterlife, but nothing happens. Instead, you hunker down in your old office to await Hannah's return tomorrow.
Turn to **228**.

76

You peer through the glass and see the headline LOCAL WOMAN IN MYSTERIOUS DEATH. You want to enter the pod to read the rest, but however hard you try, you simply cannot open the door. You look up to ask the ghost if they can help, but they have gone — scared away by the cleaner who has just arrived. They walk past, then tut and reach in to grab the newspaper. It's tossed into the bin, but luckily lies near the top, and you can read more of the article now — "ACCIDENT, SUICIDE OR MURDER?" There's also a photo of you. It's your cheesiest profile picture, taken from your LinkedIn account, and a tidal wave of sorrow washes over. You are dead. Your life is over. Even if it was a life in which LinkedIn posts mattered!

The cleaner then rattles the trolley away and the movement makes the newspaper shift down in the trash. There's nothing else you can do with that, so you head around the corner, then down a few steps into a lounge area. But before you can explore anything else, the entire office converges, then enters the conference room — there's a meeting! Turn to **225**.

77

It is creepier than you remembered, especially when you spot a ghost crow hopping up and down, dragging its broken wing along, but then you spot a small door halfway up the staircase.

That wasn't there before, you're certain, so it must be a spectral door. However, even if you could open it, you wouldn't be able to because it's phantasmagorically locked! If only you had a phantom key…

There is a **tiny 4-digit number** above the lock, so you memorise it, in case that comes in handy later, then carry on up the stairs and arrive back on the landing. Turn to **287**.

78

Trying to picture yourself talking with Adam, you clench your nostrils and give a swift blow. With a slightly painful pop in your ears, the scene transforms.

'Yes, I don't know if you've noticed—' and you immediately give a huff of annoyance. Did Adam pontificate like this all the time? Was he always so self-important? '—but Theo has been quite depressed recently. I think he's struggling with his work and now, his friend has died by suicide. He's acting as though everything is alright, but I can tell.'

You watch as the 'living you' shuffles her feet awkwardly, plainly wondering how she got into this conversation and how quickly she can extricate herself! Adam doesn't pay any attention, though.

'What I'm worried about, of course, is that suicide can beget suicide—' Did he really just say 'beget'? '—and I saw that he'd bought some paracetamol. He said it was just for a headache, but is it?'

Sensing an exit strategy, the living you pounces and says, 'Yep, I'm sure that's what it was. Anyhow, I was only looking for the mail, so…' and then you leave the office as though the hounds of Hell are chasing you.

The scene clears. Despite that being an insight into Adam's character, it's not really helping you to discover the motive for your murder, so you should carry on with your investigation.

Who's next?

> Marta   Turn to **211**
> Hannah   Turn to **72**

But if you've already done that, then drift towards the landing to think about your strategy (turn to **63**).

79

Charlie calls you over, bouncing like a hyperactive toddler and hissing, 'They're celebrating. They're celebrating! Do you think they'll have any blow?'
You can put that question on hold for now because, if you have discovered the TRUTH about Jan, you should turn to **256**. If not, turn to **11**.

80

It was the logical choice — there is literally an ESC key on it! Make a note that when you are given an opportunity to **ESCAPE** from the office, you must **add 65** to the section you are at.

However, the ESC key needs to be pressed and that's a bit more difficult. Three times you watch your entire hand sink through the keyboard and desk before wondering whether there's a way to make Adam press it. Aiming for a telepathic connection, you concentrate very hard. With your non-existent breath being held and furrowed brow, you simply look as though you're straining to go to the toilet, so it should come as no surprise when a spectral fart comes out. It's a tiny, odourless 'parp', but Adam suddenly looks around, mutters, 'What the…?' and inexplicably presses the ESC key. The ability to make the living do what you want is a useful, albeit short-lived, skill to have, so ignore the embarrassment and tick the codeword **MIASMA**.

You now feel an unpleasant pull on your intestines — or, at least, where your intestines used to be. Is this just the aftermath of your gas or did it work?

Adam then stands up, says, 'See you later,' to Theo and Robert, who's just appeared with a cup of coffee, and exits the office. And like a balloon tethered to a child, you bob along after him.

It worked! Turn to **185**.

81

You stroll around the cubicles, getting the lay of the land, but the workers ignore you. They are staring at their monitor screens and typing nonstop.

'Excuse me, what are you doing here?' you eventually ask a middle-aged man. He pushes his glasses back up to the bridge of his nose and looks up in astonishment.

'I'm working, we're all working. It's very important. We are crucial to the company's success.'

'Really?' But what are you actually doing?' And you lean forward to peer at his screen. He looks too, and then you both stare awkwardly at each other. The screen is full of never-ending gibberish.

He looks embarrassed and confused, then mutters, 'Suicide begets suicide, so he believed.'

But before you can say 'What?', he is already typing again. It's pointless trying to have a conversation with these busy workers, besides, someone is beckoning you over, and he looks like he's the boss, so you'd better obey! Turn to **117**.

82

By concentrating really hard, you make Robert close down Instagram and open up his gallery. You can see by his frown that he's either very confused by this or he heard your tiny ghost fart…

Still, you got what you wanted and watch as he swipes through his photos. And this inspired move pays off when you spot yourself! Smiling, and possibly a bit drunk, you are posing with Robert's wife — you must have been friends with her! Have you found CLUE 8? If you have, turn to **105**, but if not, turn to **247**.

83

This is an interesting suggestion — after all, Marta was annoyed when Theo took her garlic bread — but let's think this through. If you were going to teach someone a lesson about taking other people's food, wouldn't you add salt instead of sugar or a huge amount of wasabi? A deliberate overdose of paracetamol is going a bit far, don't you think?

Add 10 PURGATORY points, then turn to **150**.

84

Marta is waiting in the small corridor and pounces as soon as Adam exits the toilet.

'What were you talking to Meredith about? We had a deal!'

He looks confused at first, then wounded.

'How could you ask me that! I said I wouldn't say anything and I meant it.'

'Yes, well, being honest is not really your strong point is it. Remember, you have no proof and your word isn't actually reliable — everyone here will back me on that!'

There is a tense silence then, and even Party Ghost, who has appeared, drawn by all the drama, is watching with bated breath instead of dancing.

'So, what did you talk about then?' Marta asks in a more conciliatory tone.

'Just the presentation and my work here.'

'Oh, for the love of…' and she throws her hands up in the air. 'Would you just stop going on about the blasted presentation!'

Before Adam can even think about responding, she stalks away.
Meanwhile, people are still milling around, so there's a chance that the ghosts can notify you of anything interesting happening in their favourite areas — but only if you've **already met them and they are still here!**

> NSFW Ghost   Turn to **241**
> Charlie   Turn to **79**

But if they're not an option, then you should investigate what the COO's minion is up to.
Turn to **221**.

85

You quickly head to Louisa's office, then root around the cables while she curses about timestamps and utilisation. It is not how you thought you'd spend your afterlife but there you go. When you finally identify the WLAN, you reach out, expecting your fingers to pass through, like they've done with most other objects, but instead, grab it firmly. After a frantic few seconds, in which you can't remember the name of the HR contact, you recite a message and hope for the best.

```
Hi Louisa, we've had some further
enquiries from the police about Ashley's
death. Can you confirm the attendance of
```

all your staff on that day. Best wishes,
Melanie

You hear the message notification ping, and after a pause while Louisa reads, she then tuts and starts typing. You scramble around to read.

Hi Melanie, All in the office that day were me, Robert, Marta, Hannah and Theo. Jan was off sick and Adam took a half-day — left before lunch — for a doctor's appointment. If you need any more info, just ask. Regards, Louisa.

At first, you are just flabbergasted that it worked but eventually focus and memorise the message. This is definitely a step forward in identifying who had the opportunity to kill you!
For now, though, it's time to continue investigating the MEANS of your murder.
You head back in the kitchen, but lunch is well and truly over and the dishwasher is already running.
So, now would be a good time to talk to the other ghosts (turn to **55**).

86

You're not being serious! Marta and Jan were good friends, not just colleagues. Of course, she wasn't trying to murder him!
Add 15 PURGATORY points, then turn to **150**.

87

'I'll get straight to the point, Adam. You've got to stop this continual complaining about Theo and the bloody presentation. It's done and dusted. Theo did a great job, as he should, because he's the Team Lead. I know you don't like that. I know that you think you should have had that role, but this is the situation and, for the sake of the team, I need you to get on board.'

Phew, she's taking no prisoners today! Adam has a slight flush and is gritting his teeth, but he says nothing, just nods.

'And don't think I don't know that your doctor's appointment was made up. Robert saw you in the shopping mall!'

Still, Adam keeps silent, opting for the 'don't incriminate yourself' route, and Louisa sighs in resignation.

'You could have some good opportunities here. You could really develop your career and move into management roles, but you must stop with the lies. Now, have you got anything for this session, because I am quite busy.'

Adam can tell a dismissal when he hears one, so he agrees to draw a line under this and leaves. You make a mental note of these allegations, pleased with your investigative skills, then decide to continue while you're on a roll. Turn to **213**.

88

Easier said than done! How are you supposed to check who was in the office on a specific day? The ghosts are a waste of time when it comes to time! If only you could call up HR and ask them…

You pace around the office — past the stairs, the privacy pods, the lounge and back past the stairs — in a circuit. You are hoping for inspiration, but what happens next is beyond what you could ever have expected! Turning right after the pods, you stride down the narrow, plain corridor, only to see that, instead of the trendy exposed brickwork, there is now a door!

'Well, that's not normally there,' you say, stating the obvious. You reach out to touch it — maybe it's just a hallucination — and can feel the varnished wood under your fingertips. However, it is closed. If you have ticked the codeword ECTOPLASM and want to use this skill, turn to **297**. If you can't or won't open the door, then turn to **158**.

89

Aahh, yes, this would make sense. Reading the awful comments that Hannah made about her might have made Louisa angry enough to kill, but did she? You have to remember that Louisa gave you the promotion instead of Hannah — and that was the only revenge that Louisa needed!

Add 5 PURGATORY points, then turn to **150**.

90

By the time you've dripped the ectoplasm on the handle and squeezed through the gap, Marta is already on her phone. She frowns at the opened door, shuts it again, then continues her conversation.

'Not a chance. I don't want to raise any flags at the moment. No, don't worry. Jan knows but he's cool. And the other one that could cause trouble is being dealt with. Anyway, I better get back. See you.'
If you found CLUE 2, turn to **190**. If not, turn to **68**.

91

What? Did you think he brought poisoned curry into the office to stop you from telling his wife about the affair? Murders to silence have certainly happened, but if Robert wanted you dead, how did he get Hannah to steal it from the fridge? And why would he bring her in on the plan? And why would he get Hannah to blame it on Louisa? They were still together at that point….

Oh, there's too many questions! Plus, Robert only had glass Pyrex containers.

No, no, no, Robert did not murder you.

Add 10 PURGATORY points and turn to **150**.

92

Did you see all of them? The daffodils, banana, rubber duck, lemon, POLICE LINE tape, pina colada, and hear the songs 'Yellow Submarine' and 'Goodbye Yellow Brick Road'. Whatever happened, there is no denying the fact that they are yellow. And with that realisation, you are overwhelmed by a barrage of memories.

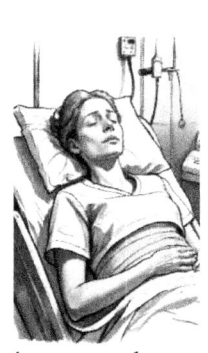

Phoning your sister and whispering that you've got the flu; your sister taking one look at your yellow skin and calling an ambulance; the emergency doctor asking how long you have been jaundiced for; the consultant palpating your liver and ominously shaking her head — you remember feeling the heavy weight in your chest as you asked, "Am I dying?" Finally, you heard your sister talking to people about you having a cold but, no, of course you wouldn't take an overdose of paracetamol*. Deliberately or accidentally! She was insistent on that, but through your half-closed eyelids, you see that the Intensive Care nurse is unconvinced.

You know you had a cold but all you remember taking was a lemon-flavoured drink remedy with paracetamol for the aches and sore throat. You'd only just opened the packet and had one, so where did the additional amount come from?

'This is why I'm still here!'

Conscripted Ghost looks quizzical, almost as if he's forgotten who you are.

'I didn't die in the office, but I must have been given the paracetamol overdose here.'
He still looks slightly baffled, and you sigh impatiently.

'Someone here poisoned me!'

Turn to **141**.

Paracetamol is the typical name used in the UK for acetaminophen.

93

It's an impersonal workplace though. Just two monitors, docking station, keyboard and mouse adorn the surface. No photos, no fidget toys, no unwashed cups, nothing. But then you spot a cactus perched on the adjacent set of three drawers that the man is rummaging through…

'Trevor! Trevor the prickly pear!' and with a blow of utter sadness, you realise that this was your desk. Tick the codeword **TREVOR**.

You slump into the chair that is adjusted specifically for your height, even though you can't actually feel the cushion underneath.

Maybe there were other personal items, but they've been cleared away. Did your loved ones collect them as mementos? Do you have any loved ones?

But you still do not have the answers to these questions. You don't even know what your job was?

Your curiosity breaks through the melancholia, and you lean forward to see what the man is looking at. Clearly, not everything has been tidied up — you spot random teabags, half-used pens, a pack of flu drink powders, lozenges and not one but two packets of tissues! The man grumbles and slams the drawer closed before opening the bottom one. Deodorant, an umbrella, an unopened multipack of Bounty bars and a half-eaten bar of milk chocolate come into view. He grimaces at the Bounty bars but grabs the milk chocolate, breaks off a chunk, then with his cheek bulging, leaves this office. Tick **CLUES 7 and 10**.

You try to open the top drawer, but your hand passes straight through, which doesn't make sense, seeing as you haven't passed through the chair, but what do you know about being dead? The top drawer will have to remain a mystery, although, judging from the contents of the others, it's probably not enlightening. Apparently, you were a messy, sweaty chocoholic with a runny nose!

Suddenly, the door opens again and, with a clatter of high, yet professional, heels, a young woman enters the office, then plonks her bag on the other desk. She swiftly brings out a laptop, then sits down. No prevaricating for her — she's straight down to business! If only you knew who she was…

Next, you could look out of the window (turn to **186**) or check out the other (now-occupied) desk (turn to **237**).

94

Her head swings awkwardly over her shoulder as she shudders with shock.

'You've been down to the basement? Did you see the mangled one?'

You nod, then add, 'He seems alright. Not frightening at all, once you chat with him. Just don't look too closely at the injuries if they bother you…'

And you wonder about reminding Clara that she's no oil painting herself but then realise that she's already gone. So, you continue up to the landing. Turn to **287**.

95

You rush down to the creepy back stairs, key clasped tightly in your transparent hand. It fits, and as though by magic, the door clicks open to reveal…

A skeleton! And not just any skeleton, but one that has a huge hole blown out of the back of its skull. Almost as if the poor person had shot themselves. You've already met the ghost to whom these earthly remains belong, and the next time you meet them, you should tell them that you've discovered their bones. To do that, you'll need to remember this section number: **95**.

For now, though, you close the door, resealing the skeleton in its cobweb-strewn tomb, then head back upstairs.

You must return to your previous section, which was either **224** or **258**.

96

Your knowledge of Theo's corporate theft would have been ample motive for him to silence you, but it seems that you didn't know anything. No wonder he was so relieved! Turn to **173**.

97

You enter your old office, automatically quietening when you see that Hannah is on the phone, before remembering that she can't hear or see you at all. And as you stand there, your eyes are drawn again to the prickly pear, which is why you spot a folded-up scrap of paper that is resting against the ceramic pot. A scrap of paper that flutters open when you poke it — it's a spectral message!

> Hello, Yellow New Ghost.
> I remembered something that might help.
> Whoops-a-daisy, number 3.
> Love, Monica. April 1975

At first, you're taken aback by the audacity of your new nickname. Yellow New Ghost!! But then you focus your attention on the actual message. What is it supposed to mean?

However, before you can make any progress, Hannah suddenly stands up, mutters about stale air, and switches on the fan, swirling you away.

Once you've collected yourself together, you make a mental note of Monica's strange advice. Although you don't realise it yet, this is rather useful information. When you hear anyone say the words **Whoops-a-daisy**, you must immediately **multiply** the section you are on by **3**, then turn to that new section. You will NOT be prompted to do this, so keep your wits about you!

With nothing else to do here, you leave the office. Turn to **144**.

98

It's not a success, that has to be said. You groan, moan and even try a howl, but the only thing that happens is that the fridge makes a mechanical whine, so Theo opens the door up, shouting, 'I think the fridge is on its last legs, Hannah.' Moments later, though, he's smiling and pocketing the lone spring roll that he found.

'That'll do for later. Shame there's no chilli dipping sauce. I wonder whose it was…'

Tick **CLUE 10**. You feel quite exhausted after that effort, but you could drag yourself back to the office to examine the desk he had been searching (turn to **215**). If you'd prefer, you could just stay here with Theo — is he going to do any work today? — and see what happens next (turn to **18**).

99

The words 'whoops-a-daisy' ring a bell. Is that what Monica meant in her note? And without truly knowing what you're doing, you find yourself heading to the stairs — to the treacherous, dangerous stairs, and three steps down, you hear the creak of a warped plank. You have no problem in prising the wood up and in the space of the tread, there is a pair of shoes.

As you perch there, staring at them, Clara the maid appears.

'That was the step I tripped on. The step that made me fall down and break my neck. I never knew that it was a hidey-hole…'

You turn to ask her more about the accident and the strange shoes, but Clara's voice has gone wispy. She is merging into a beam of strong, white light that has appeared in the entrance foyer of the offices, and before your very eyes, she becomes a trillion photons and is gone.

Subtract 10 PURGATORY points and if **Clara** was on your Met-A-Ghost list, you must now **strike her off**.

You are stunned and a little teary. Pleased for Clara — she has moved on to… wherever — but sad for your own relentless existence here. How long will it be before you can move on?

But there's no point in self-pity, so you pick up the **phantom shoes** and plan your next step.

Do you want to visit the boss woman now? If you do, turn to **269**; however, if you've already spied on her, then your next move depends on whether you've ticked the codeword TELEPORTATION. If you have, turn to **259** and if not, turn to **13**.

100

The days pass by, fellow ghosts come and go, and at one point you hear the New Year's Eve fireworks and notice that they are heralding in 2031! But you've only been dead a week, haven't you? Time is, indeed, a bit strange here, so maybe you should start again and see if you can find more clues the next time around.

You can keep the acquired clues, codewords, objects and ghosts; just **add 10 PURGATORY** points, then turn to **1**.

101

Are you joking? Theo and Hannah got on well enough, and he had no reason at all to kill her.
Add 15 PURGATORY points, then turn to **150**.

102

Of course, Theo used to steal food all the time. Surely, if Adam left some unclaimed food in the fridge, Theo couldn't help himself — he would eat it without a flicker of a guilty conscience. And then Adam could hint that Theo actually meant to take his own life, seeing as his close friend, Danesh, had also died of a paracetamol overdose. Oh, it could have been so neat, so easy. So, what went wrong?

If you have ticked CLUE 7, turn to **60**. If not, turn to **280**.

103

Presumably, it was a nice service but seeing as you fell asleep (or whatever it is that ghosts do), you missed it and only come around when Adam is leaving and saying a few words to your relatives.

'I'll miss her so much. She was such a good friend. We were thinking of setting up our own start-up business, you know, she was just so in awe of my programming.'

At that point, he is shunted away by the backlog of grievers, but you hear your relatives say, 'Who was that? Someone Ashley worked with?'

However much you'd like to stay and listen to their side of this, you are linked to Adam and when he goes to the car park, you go too. It's an awkward meeting between him, Jan and Louisa — they can hardly ignore each other! — but while Adam is explaining that he is cycling back to the office as it is such a nice day, you spot a strange woman who is staring in your direction. You look around to see what's caught her eye and notice a group of battered, tattered musicians. Maybe you've got enough time to go and investigate one of these oddities, but who? The strange woman (turn to **160**) or the musicians (turn to **273**)?

104

You've never experienced a fireside chat before, but it seems to be poorly named. There is no fireside, and instead of a chat, it's a one-way lecture from Meredith! Maybe she is jetlagged because she cuts through the usual niceties to announce that the London office is being closed. There is a collective gasp and Jan laughs. With an aggrieved tone, she then says that, because of the UK employment laws, there will be redundancy packages or people could relocate to the States. It's a lot to take in!

'I'm sure you've got plenty of questions, so let's get the food and we can go over everything while we eat.' Meredith is already striding to the door before she's finished speaking — clearly, she wants this to be done and dusted!

'Good Lord,' a voice mutters beside you. It's Conscripted Ghost. 'Talking while eating. I do hope none of them choke. Then we'll never get rid of them!'

It's a good point, but maybe you have just remembered something very important that you had to share with this particular spectre. Something that you found when you used a key to open the phantasmagorically locked door…

If so, you were told of a number to memorise, and you should now **ADD** that to this section number and turn *immediately* to the new number.

If not, you are more concerned that the window of opportunity for finding your killer is closing fast. You can't investigate an empty office!

But maybe you have found all the clues and learnt all you need to know; it's time to put your money where your mouth is! Turn to **127**.

105

'And he's having an affair with Louisa!' you announce in the shocked tones of a Victorian spinster. Instantly, the obvious suspicion bursts in your mind — did he silence you so that you couldn't tell his wife about his philandering? Now that would be a reasonable motive for murder! With this excitement, you've lost your concentration and Robert closes the photos and puts his phone down. Nevertheless, you have discovered the **TRUTH about Robert**.

The next interviewee is coming in, so you decide to sneak through the gap to see what Theo is doing now (turn to **192**).

106

You frown, then ignore Charlie. Marta and Jan's conversation is much more interesting…

'So, when do you start?'

'They want me to do the onboarding at the start of next month.'

'Wow, that's not long for Louisa to find your replacement. She's going to be furious!'

'Serves her right. She could've altered my notice period after the probation time, but she didn't. She wanted to be able to get rid of me as quick as possible; well, that works both ways!'

'And so soon after the interviews for Ashley's old position — sucks to be the boss!'

And they both laugh, cackling with Schadenfreude!

'Talking of Ashley,' Marta says, 'She would have been pleased. I told you she knew about your job search but never grassed us up to Louisa.'

'Because she wanted me out of here! It was not thanks to the good of her heart!'

'Whatever! Anyway, all's well that ends well.'

And they head out of the office to see what's happening with the Head Office bigwigs.

Meanwhile, you could check in with the other ghosts, but only if you've **already met them**.

> NSFW Ghost   Turn to **241**
> Pale Ghost   Turn to **122**

But if they're not an option, you can investigate what the COO's minion is up to. Turn to **221**.

107

With a quick glance, you see that the interviews are being held in the conference room with Louisa and Robert.

'Poor sods,' you mutter and give a theatrical shudder, even though no one can appreciate it. The candidates — three, so far — are sitting in the lounge, wearing their finest professional outfits and clutching briefcases. Theo is lurking around, and you know that he's trying to look welcoming and helpful, while really, he's just skiving! Do you want to haunt the conference room (turn to **236**) or eavesdrop on Theo (turn to **29**)?

108

But the office is empty. You drift aimlessly around the desks, looking for inspiration, when suddenly, you see a young man, lying on the floor. It's Charlie with glazed, open eyes and a trickle of blood from a head wound. Just as you bend over to get a better look, the corpse sneezes white powder in your face, then leaps to his feet.

'Sorry about that. It just happens sometimes. What are you doing? Have you—'
Luckily, his rapid-fire stream of consciousness is interrupted by the return of Marta. And she's carrying a cheap burgundy Tupperware bowl with a homemade stir fry in it. Charlie, temporarily stunned into silence, watches her while she eats, then says, 'Do you want to photocopy your bum now?'

Blimey, he's obsessed! But you need to keep him on your side for now, so you decline politely and ask, 'Have you seen Jan with any food or Tupperware?' He thinks, rubbing his nose and sniffing.

'No. I think he always goes out at lunchtime. But when they are here, they're really sneaky, as though they've got a secret. And they talk all the time about indeed and monsters!' Tick **CLUE 3**. He smiles and nods repeatedly, until you ask who.

'Jan and Marta, Jan and Marta. Do you think they're having an affair? Do you think they're at it?' You sigh — it's like talking to a teenage boy! — then drift out of the office. Well, Charlie's gossip could be useful, although it's nothing to do with food… You need to stay focused on "means", so what should you do next? You could talk to:

NSFW Ghost	Turn to **243**
Beehive Ghost	Turn to **175**
Party Ghost	Turn to **208**

…but only if you've **previously met them**!

And if you've finished with the spectres, then you could check out the kitchen for any clues (turn to **35**), but if you've already done that, then tick the codeword **MEANS** and think about the next stage of your investigation.

If you've ticked the codeword OPPORTUNITY, turn to **246**, if not, turn to **6**.

109

Conscripted Ghost watches as you wrestle with the conundrum, then begins to repeatedly sink then rise through the chair out of boredom. Nice trick, you think, wondering if you could do it too. However, this prevarication is just avoiding the truth — you have no idea what the answer is. Maybe you could have another look around or maybe there is somewhere that you haven't visited yet. With a gasp, you sit bolt upright and shout, 'The toilets!'

If you've ticked the codeword ECTOPLASM, turn to **289**, but if you haven't, turn to **100**.

110

He blusters for a few seconds, looks confused, then finally says, 'That's not me!'

Oh well, Robert was the wrong choice.

Although you're quite happy to continue with the bingo, too many people are moving around this small space, making both time and the surroundings shift and judder. By the time everything settles again, Louisa is announcing the next activity. Turn to **275**.

111

It's not a terrible suggestion — silencing a witness to save your own skin is a common reason for murder — but it's not the case here. Marta was not worried that you knew about her thieving.

Add 5 PURGATORY points, then turn to **150**.

112

You peer over her shoulder, making her shiver with the sudden chill, and read the first statement.

Got a first-class honours degree

You and Marta both hum as you weigh up the possibilities. Who do you think Marta should talk to first? Who do you think is the clever clogs?

Hannah	Turn to **27**
Adam	Turn to **293**
Jan	Turn to **239**
Robert	Turn to **110**
Theo	Turn to **166**

113

You're absolutely convinced that you know where the prize is and glide through the office until reaching the privacy pods. However, Robert and Adam must have gone somewhere else! Seconds later, you hear a triumphant shout and realise that they found the prize and you didn't!

There's no time to be peeved about it though, as Louisa is wrapping up the team bonding session. And not a moment too soon. She looks like she's going to spend her lunch break in the nearest wine bar! Everyone heads either to their desks or the toilet, and you end up floating aimlessly in the large, vaulted office. Turn to **214**.

114

There were definitely stalker-like hints about Adam's feelings for you — maybe you rejected his advances and he reacted with the classic "If I can't have you, no one can!"

Actually, though, Adam's declarations were only made to elevate his own sense of importance and had no groundings in reality at all. He was simply using your death as a way of getting attention. Besides, what part did Hannah play in his dastardly plan? Surely, he couldn't have known that she was going to take the food, thinking it was actually Louisa's, and give it to you! No, that doesn't make sense!

Add 5 PURGATORY points, then turn to **195**.

115

This feels familiar. The mid-afternoon slump of energy. Staring at a screen and willing the clock to shift rapidly to a time when you can finally shut down and leave, but it just ticks by so slowly.

'Not having to do any work is one benefit of being dead, I suppose,' you remark to the ether.

'You don't sound convinced of that. Have you found out nothing yet?'

It's Chain-Smoking Ghost again and despite the nonstop cigarettes, you're pleased to have some company. You shrug in answer to his question, then ask, 'Is there really a Heaven and Hell?'

Instead of that opening up an interesting conversation, Chain-Smoking Ghost just snorts and floats away, muttering, 'Women! Should stay at home! Stupid, the lot of them!'

Make that Chain-Smoking *SEXIST* Ghost…

With nothing else to do, you decide to visit the parts of the office you've not yet explored. It's not a great choice, but do you want to visit the server room (turn to **19**) or the storeroom (turn to **203**)?

116

She tries to keep quiet, but Louisa has a nagging thought that she can't leave alone. A thought concerning someone she used to work with…

'Did Ashley ever talk about me? About my previous job?'

It's an odd pair of questions, which immediately sounds suspicious, but after a moment of confusion, your mum stares Louisa directly in the eyes.

'Ashley didn't like the way you treated Jan. I mean, she didn't like Jan by the end, but she always said there was no need for you to behave the way you did with him just because he's Polish.'

There is another long, drawn-out silence until Louisa asks, 'Did Ashley mention Astrid Pomeroy?'

'What?' And your mum looks completely bamboozled by the question. It's enough for Louisa to sigh with relief and usher her out. When she returns to her office, she sinks into the chair, muttering, 'Thank goodness, I didn't do anything more drastic than giving an underqualified person a job. She didn't even know about my history with Astrid!'

Despite bristling that she's called you 'under-qualified' — how dare she! — you desperately want to hear a lengthier confession from Louisa, but she then strides out of the office to see what's happening with the Head Office bigwigs.
Meanwhile, you could check in with the other ghosts, but only if you've **already met them**.

> Charlie   Turn to **79**
> Pale Ghost   Turn to **122**

But if they're not an option, then you should investigate what the COO's minion is up to.
Turn to **221**.

117

The boss has practically wasted away. His flesh is as thin as paper and clings tightly to his skeleton, while the clothes hang loosely off his frame. Here is a man who lost weight fast, and you think it's obvious what he died of. This momentarily distracts you, as you remember that you're still yellow from the jaundice, but he interrupts with a sharp, 'Yes?'

    'Hello, I'm recently dead and worked in the other office. I didn't know this place was here. What are you doing?'

    'Working. Busy, busy, busy.'

    Did you work so hard that you ignored your health issues?'

His façade crumbles at little with your directness and he nods.

'Had a cough for months, voice went hoarse, lost weight. Just put it down to stress.'

'And now you wish you'd spent that time with family instead of the office?'

'You presumptuous little minx!' He wheezes, banging a fist on his desk. 'The only regret I have is that I didn't get to complete the merger before the lung cancer got me! I even took the files into the hospice.'

After a pause for Workaholic Ghost to get his breath (what was left of it) back, he asks, 'But you can make yourself useful while you're here. I've lost something under the desk. Have you got a torch?'

It's a strange request — maybe it's something to do with 'going towards the light' or maybe you've just watched too many ghost movies — but if you have found a torch, turn to **231**, and if not, turn to **140**.

118

Adam storms into Louisa's office after only a cursory knock. She is shocked, hastily closing the shopping website she was on before shouting, 'What on Earth do you think you're doing?'

'This is a formal complaint. It is bad enough that Theo is designated my superior despite his obvious failings, but I do not see why I have to tolerate his threats and insults!'

At first, Louisa is dumbstruck, then asks, 'What failings?' Having to explicitly pin down his grievances is something that Adam wasn't expecting, but he rises admirably to the occasion.

'The presentation to management was not as good as it could have been. I had prepared a detailed slide stack and would have demonstrated both passion and excellence — something that Theo is incapable of!'

'We've already talked about this, Adam. The presentation went well. Management was very impressed. I really think you need to rethink things here before we take it further.'

The veiled warning is clear to hear and Adam has, at least, the common sense to heed it. He gives a curt nod of the head, then retreats, all anger deflated. That might have been an enlightening encounter, but if you're going to get the truth, you need to head back to Robert, And it's clear that you must increase the fear factor!

Have you acquired a pair of phantom shoes? If you have, turn to **153**, but if not, turn to **49**.

119

You peer over his shoulder, watching as a brief spasm of pain twitches his neck, and read the first statement.

Sent someone flowers last week

You and Adam both blow your cheeks out as you weigh up the possibilities. Who do you think Adam should talk to first? Who do you think is the romantic?

Hannah	Turn to **27**
Robert	Turn to **205**
Jan	Turn to **239**
Marta	Turn to **194**
Theo	Turn to **166**

120

With your nose held and a swift blow, you concentrate on the reasons why Hannah might hate you enough to poison you. Suddenly, your ears pop, and the scene transforms.

It's you! And you're sitting at your desk, reading a message. Hannah isn't there, but judging by the way you look sneakily around, she's not gone far and you're definitely up to something!

The message is from Hannah and about a meeting that Louisa was going to set up but obviously didn't. Hannah is livid — "so annoyed", "incompetence" and "can't organise a **** in a brewery!" — but what you see next is much, much worse…

Seconds later, you've printed out a screenshot of the message and left it on Louisa's desk. You squirm as you watch yourself run back to your desk, smirk and mutter, 'That should see off the competition!' And then the scene fades. Tick **CLUE 9**.

Did you really do that? What a horrible person! And, more importantly, did Hannah know that you'd done it? That would be a bona fide motive for murder, and if you have ticked CLUE 1, turn immediately to **34**. If not, continue reading.

While you're taking all this in, you float out of the office and can now check out Adam (turn to **278**) or Marta (turn to **211**). But if you've already done that, then drift towards the landing to think about your strategy (turn to **63**).

121

And you watch as Louisa scrutinises the 'likes' and sees your tiny profile photo. She doesn't say anything, just harrumphs. Is this her motive? Did you know she was racist and she was worried that you'd reveal her dismissal from another job over it? That probably would be a good reason to get rid of you, but wouldn't it have been easier to just sack you? Less police involvement, surely!

You have discovered the **TRUTH about Louisa**.

You feel a bit sick — finding tangible evidence that someone might have murdered you is enough to upset anyone's stomach — but Louisa is finished now.

'You look a bit green. Under all that yellow, I mean.'

You shriek and spin around to face NSFW Ghost, who has materialised behind you. If you haven't done so yet, record that you have met **NSFW GHOST**. He's so close he could touch and in fact…

'Keep your distance, you pervert!'

He gives a good-natured grin, then shrugs as he withdraws his groping hand.

'Well, if I had something that entertained me, I wouldn't have to sneak up on women, would I?'

You're tempted to lecture him about harassment in the workplace, then wonder whether you do actually have something. If you have found a spectral newspaper and want to give it to him, turn to **285**, but if you don't have one or don't feel so generous, you could visit the weaselly man now (turn to **216**). However, if you've already spied on him, then your next move depends on whether you've ticked the codeword TELEPORTATION. If you have ticked it, turn to **259** and if not, turn to **13**.

122

Pale Ghost beckons you with a weak wave, saying, 'He requested a one-to-one with the boss. It sounds very important.'

And yet, Meredith has gone to fetch a coffee, so Adam is waiting in the lounge area. He's trying to look self-assured, like he talks to the CEO every day, but the frequent, nervous lip-licking is a giveaway. Finally, she returns.

'So, er, Adam, is it? What can I do for you?'
He takes a deep breath in through his nose.

'It's a challenge to get noticed here; to get rewarded for good work. I've tried raising it in my quarterly reviews, but nothing changes. For example, we had a client meeting that could have led to a significant deal, but despite my PowerPoint being more superior in terms of detail and engagement, Theo was allowed to take lead on it. It simply isn't fair to be overlooked, again and again.'

After the long, rambling rant ends, Meredith stares at him. You can't tell if she's impressed with his brazenness or dumbfounded that he thinks this is appropriate, but eventually, she says, 'But Theo is the Team Lead…'

Adam stares back, swallows, then stammers, 'Well, yes, right, OK, thanks,' while nodding furiously, and before the blush of pure humiliation can consume him, he walks swiftly to the toilets.

Ouch! That was quite the burn! If you have discovered the TRUTH about Marta, turn now to **128**. If not, you should get a move on — the Head Office bigwigs have started to wander over to the Conference Room — the 'fireside chat' is about to start! Turn to **104**.

123

But as you approach, there is a nauseating swirl of air, then a woman appears. She's wearing a mustard-coloured dress and huge glasses.

'Just arrived, I suppose,' she states before sitting at the desk. A typewriter has also materialised and is weirdly superimposed over the keyboard that is already on the desk. She tuts, mutters about this newfangled nonsense getting in the way, then introduces herself.

Record that you have met **MONICA**.

You have to shout over the noise of her loud clacking as she starts typing with an impressive speed.

'Do you know what I should do now?'

Monica stops, lights a cigarette and after she's blown out a lungful of smoke, gestures to the other desk. You look over and spot the sad-looking cactus, sensing a spark of recognition. Tick the codeword **TREVOR**.

'I know you. That was your desk, wasn't it, but I don't remember seeing you die here.'

'When did you last see me?'

'A while. Maybe a century…'

You scoff and she shrugs apologetically. 'Time's a bit strange here. It's hard to keep track of it. You had a nasty cold, though. I remember that. Sniffing and sneezing. Did you die of that?'

You shrug, wishing that some memories would flood back but, so far, there is nothing.

'How did you die? If it's not rude to ask…'

She smiles, obviously delighted to share the details, then leans over to the plug socket. A blast of blue light shoots out, the lights flicker and Monica's hair stands on end.

'A split second and that was that! Faulty wiring in the plug, but I overheard my boss telling the police that I didn't understand the equipment, so I caused the electrocution myself. And the police were satisfied with it!"

'Didn't you complain?' But as soon as the words are spoken, you realise how powerless you are now. Monica could have complained till the cows came home, but what difference could a silent, invisible ghost make?

Suddenly, the door opens and, with a clatter of high, yet professional, heels, a young woman enters the office. Monica vanishes, sneering her disapproval, as the newcomer plonks her bag on the desk, brings out a laptop, then sits down. No prevaricating for her — she's straight down to business! If only you knew who she was…

You could now check out the other desk that the man was looking in (turn to **171**) or peek out of the window (turn to **186**).

124

The green algae finally decides that this is the perfect time to slide off your ethereal skin. And like a chalk etching of a gravestone, it smears over the wall, highlighting the drawing that you'd never noticed before.

Head to **Appendix C** (What the CAUL reveals) at the back of the book to study the drawing, then return **here** afterwards.

It must be some sort of puzzle, but what does it mean? Surely, it's a cryptic clue to your murder, and you're in the office, so maybe it has something to do with office things like your computer…

What do you want to examine closely on your computer?

Search browser	Turn to **226**
Emails	Turn to **161**
Office apps	Turn to **20**

125

What's the theory? That Marta was defending her friend, Jan, against the incessant discrimination from Louisa? It's not ringing true, is it? Besides, Marta was helping Jan, but in a more practical way, by writing a first-class reference for him. She didn't need to kill Louisa.

Add 5 PURGATORY points, then turn to **150**.

126

You are the first to reach the kitchen and immediately stick your face into the fridge — three Tupperware containers, one green and two burgundies — plus one fancy glass Pyrex tub. Now all you have to do is wait.

And you don't have to wait too long before Marta comes to retrieve the cheap burgundy Tupperware, but then Robert arrives. He takes the Pyrex and nukes it in the microwave, releasing a pungent odour of hot bacon! And suddenly, there is a commotion from the lounge area. A crackling, thudding noise. It sounds like a burning boar is hurling itself from wall to wall! If you want to investigate this, turn to **42**, but if you'd prefer to stay in the kitchen to see who picks up the remaining green and burgundy Tupperware, turn to **191**.

127

You can rule out Hannah — she gave you the curry, thinking that it was Louisa's food and the boss would be angry at you for taking it. A simple tit-for-tat in revenge for your interview sabotage. But someone else had actually brought it into the office and put it in the fridge with its deadly addition. The question is: Who did that?

Robert	Turn to **2**
Louisa	Turn to **235**
Marta	Turn to **165**
Jan	Turn to **229**
Adam	Turn to **61**
Theo	Turn to **272**

128

Marta is waiting in the small corridor and pounces as soon as Adam exits the toilet.

'What were you talking to Meredith about? We had a deal!'

He looks confused at first, then wounded.

'How could you ask me that! I said I wouldn't say anything and I meant it.'

'Yes, well, being honest is not really your strong point is it. Remember, you have no proof and your word isn't actually reliable — everyone here will back me on that!'

There is a tense silence then and even Party Ghost, who has appeared, apparently drawn by all the drama, is watching with bated breath instead of dancing.

'So, what did you talk about then?' Marta asks in a more conciliatory tone.

'Just the presentation and my work here.'

'Oh, for the love of…' and she throws her hands up in the air. 'Would you just stop going on about the blasted presentation!'

Before Adam can respond, a fraught-looking Justin approaches, and tells them that the fireside chat is about to start, so you all head quickly to the Conference Room. Turn to **104**.

129

Through an archway and down a couple of steps, you arrive at an open-plan lounge area. It's all plants, curved lines and brand colours. A couple of chairs and padded banks are determined to give the impression that this is a place where great ideas are created, but in a caring, collaborative way! In the corner of this space, there is a glass-walled office — contained but still transparent — and the woman is sitting at the desk. Having the single office earmarks her as being the boss, although she must hate the lack of privacy. You watch as she surreptitiously sniffs her armpits, then grabs a bottle of perfume from a drawer, liberally squirting herself, before applying more lipstick.

'Looking good, Louisa,' she tells herself, obviously not knowing that she's being observed by you AND the ghost who's perched on the edge of her desk. Luckily, she has left the door open, so you squeeze through and introduce yourself. The spectre nods back, but it's half-hearted. He seems to be very disinterested, but then you see that his hand is down the front of his trousers and realise what his preoccupation is.

'What are you doing?'

In hindsight, this is a stupid thing to say, as it's clear as day what he's doing, plus you sound like a prude.

'Oh, come on. We'd only just got the internet. What else was I going to do? Mind you, in my time, this office had proper walls, so you could get away with watching naughty stuff then. That was until I had a heart attack. Very embarrassing. Credit to them, though. They zipped me back up and didn't tell my wife. You're new, aren't you?'

'Yes, but I haven't a clue about anything. How I died, where I died, why I'm here…'

You must look quite pathetic because he hops off the desk, walks around the woman, who is now reading emails on her laptop, and grabs you by the shoulders. You give a quick glance of disgust at his hands — after all, you know where they've been! — then look back at his face. He's got an earnest expression and says, 'Ectoplasm!'

'Excuse me?'

'It took me forever to learn things here, but I will help you. And you'll definitely need ectoplasm.'

He lets go, then holds out his hand. A small glob of mucus starts to hang down off his fingertip in a perfect teardrop, and you feel slightly queasy. It's not… is it? It can't be! Oh, that's sick! As if he's read your mind, he snaps, 'No, it's not THAT. It's ectoplasm. Just hold a digit out and it'll start to pool up then drip off. And the key thing is, any door handle you drop it on will open. It's the only way to get through closed doors, seeing as we can't actually walk through walls! Good, eh?'

Well, it's better than nothing, so tick the codeword **ECTOPLASM** and record that you have met **NSFW GHOST**.

Before he can tell you anything else, Louisa stands up and leaves the office. However, she's only heading to the kitchen for a cup of coffee, so you decide to continue exploring in the hope that something, somewhere will trigger a memory. Would you like to go downstairs (turn to **177**), along the landing (turn to **230**) or right down the narrow corridor (turn to **32**)?

130

You watch with a mixture of fascination and disgust as the white ooze swells up from your right thumb, then quickly smear it on the handle before it drips onto the carpet tiles. A quiet click, and you are inside the server room. A sudden memory hits you — you were in here once before when the internet inexplicably died and a group of you squeezed in to stare at the router. Nobody knew what they were doing, of course, and the internet returned on its own accord after half an hour — however, you're absolutely certain that it wasn't this hot! Phantom sweat immediately pours down your face, and you swear your skin is starting to tighten like crispy bacon. Old-fashioned brass sconces are softening under the intense heat, becoming Picasso-like deformities on the wall. You have to get out! But the ectoplasm sizzles the second it emerges, so you sink to your knees in despair, wondering whether you can actually suffer a second death. Predictably though, the heat fades and in its place is a lovely smell. Lemongrass and coconut, you realise, imagining your stomach growl at the prospect of some Thai cuisine. Such is the way of your new existence that this smell also disappears, so you decide to leave.

If you want to visit the storeroom now, turn to **147**, but if you have already been there, turn to **277**.

131

Of course, the boiler room reminds you of Freddy Kruger, which does not help your nerves, but other than an ominous rattling and thudding of pipes, the area seems to be normal and harmless. There must be a caretaker, because he or she has left a newspaper perched on the handle of an iron valve. However, when you look closer, you realise that not only is it a tabloid edition from 1983, but you can pick it up too! Make a note that you have found a **spectral newspaper**! The hot, stifling air is getting too much for you, despite the fact that you are not even breathing!

You decide to head back upstairs, but do you want to go via the normal stairs (turn to **260**) or the creepy, not-often-used back staircase (turn to **77**)?

132

Almost as if he's in a trance, Jan stops halfway down the stairs, sits on the step, gets his laptop out and presses the ESC key. You immediately feel the unpleasant tug in your guts and, tethered to Jan, you venture out into Marylebone Station.

He heads down to the Bakerloo line, and you keep close to him, avoiding the surge of bodies that pass by. He must sense you, though, because he rubs the back of his neck as though suffering from a cramp.

Before long, you both exit at Piccadilly Circus and he enters a nearby office block. Once in the lift, he buttons his collar up and puts a tie on. You can feel his nervousness — a slight tremor through your bowel — and realise that he's going for an interview!

'And why are you leaving your current post, Mr Zapalska?

'There are some personality issues, which have been addressed but haven't improved, so I'd like to move on. I normally love my job and want to feel this again.'

There is a weird tension with these words and you snigger in recognition. Jan does not love his job at all, but the things you have to say in interviews. Suddenly, you have a flashback to stating categorically how passionate you were about social media! That wasn't so long ago — your interview for the Marketing Lead job — but it worked because you got the promotion and not Hannah. And then there is a tiny niggle inching around your mind. No, that's not the whole story, is it? But what are you forgetting…? Tick **CLUE 1**.

By the time, you've refocused, Jan has left the building and is tucked in a doorway on his phone. You somehow squeeze between his ear and the phone so you can hear both sides.

'I think it went well. And they quoted from the reference. Seemed impressed, so thanks for that. If I get this job, I owe you!'

'At least it went better than the last one.'

'Yes, although that was a success just for getting me out of the office on that day. A bad interview is still a good alibi. Look, you're sure that the boss hasn't got a clue about this?'

'Not a bit. She's happy when you're not here. You know she probably would give you a great reference, just to get rid of you, so she can fill your position with a native!' Tick **CLUE 6**.

Suddenly, you feel nauseous, but when you try to press a hand against your stomach, you realise that it has vanished. And so has your right foot. And left shoulder. And your lower jaw! The only thing you can think of before your mind starts to disintegrate, is that you've been out of the office for too long. Tick the codeword **TELEPORTATION**, then turn to **264**.

133

Louisa walks across the lounge area and back into her office. You watch as Robert waits for the others to go, then follows her like a lost puppy. There is a faint hint of annoyance on her face when he stands in her doorway, but Robert is oblivious.

'We could have gone together, had lunch somewhere afterwards. We could talk things through, sort it out—' Tick **CLUE 8**.

'For Heaven's sake. I told you on Sunday, it's over. We have careers to think about. You have a marriage and family to think about. Get a grip and go and do some work!'

Robert stands there, gaping like a goldfish. He looks hurt but simmering underneath is a humiliated fury. You wouldn't want to get on his wrong side, you think, then wonder if you *did* get on his wrong side? When Robert strops away, Louisa watches him with an aggrieved frown and then begins to look through the calendar on her computer.

It looks like she's preparing to leave soon, so you better be ready to go with her. Except you've watched enough films to know that ghosts can't escape from their place of haunting. Unless, that is, you've learnt a trick from Clara the maid…

If you haven't yet met the ghost called Clara, then you are going to have to abandon any thoughts of attending your own funeral and must turn to **233**.

But if you have, then turn to **Appendix A** (What's on the Desk?) at the back of the book and choose the item that is the solution to Clara's riddle. When you have made your selection and noted its associated number, **return here**.

You must now **ADD the number** to this section, then turn to the new section. If it begins with "It was the logical choice...", then you have chosen correctly, but if not, accept defeat and turn to **233**.

134
There really wasn't any evidence that Robert hated Theo enough to kill him!
Add 15 PURGATORY points, then turn to **150**.

135

This impotence makes your temper boil over and you have a tantrum in the middle of the lounge area. Stamping your feet (silently), making rude gestures (invisibly) and weirdest of all, emanating a smell of burnt garlic…

At this point, the conference door opens and everyone hushes. Which is why you hear one of the interviewees murmurs, 'What is that stink?' but there is no time to congratulate yourself on this manifestation. Every second counts, so you decide to see how these interviews are going. Turn to **236**.

136

It's not a success, that has to be said. And it's not even as if your fingers go through the unwashed glass; you simply split and go around it. Luckily, once you've dragged your hand back and cursed with frustration, you magically reform but then notice something odd. Theo is in a trance and singing again. Is it connected to your failed attempt at phantom telekinesis?

"Oh, I've finally decided my future lies, beyond the… ah, ah, aaahh" He continues to tunelessly wail for a while before coming back to his senses. You're certain that you know that song too, but just can't recall its **title**. In fact, you feel quite exhausted after that effort, but you could drag yourself back to the office to examine the desk he had been searching (turn to **215**).

If you'd prefer, you could just stay here with Theo — is he going to do any work today? — and see what happens next (turn to **18**).

137

While it's true that you can never really tell what goes on behind closed doors, you're sure that Louisa didn't feel any need to defend herself against Robert. Her entire demeanour and the fact that she casually dumped him after your death show that!

Add 10 PURGATORY points, then turn to **150**.

138

'I heard about you,' says the ghost with an almost-accusatory tone. At first, you are too taken aback to reply — after all, her scalp has been half-ripped off and is currently flapping against the side of her neck, blood-drenched hair wrapped around her arm. She notices your stare and scoffs.

'Oh, this? Those new printing presses, wouldn't you know it. Got me hair caught in it and with a whizz, off came me scalp. Died a couple of hours later, from shock and blood loss, they said. The hospital was very nice though. Mind you, you'd know that, wouldn't you? It was where you died.'

You gape, then mouth some random words, before eventually asking, 'How do you know that?' and the Scalped Ghost mimes something with her hands.

'You know, the magical pocket thing. One of the cleaners was showing the chatty woman it — I think it was your obituary, but I don't know how they got a newspaper in the small thing — anyway, they said that there were to be no flowers just donations to the hospital.'

Ah-ha, this is very interesting news. OK, so you still don't know what you died of in the hospital or why you are haunting the office, but it's a step forward. Or should that be a glide forward…

Suddenly, the cleaner barrels down the corridor, and their cart ploughs straight into the ghost. She is swirled into oblivion, while you float up and out of danger.

Record that you have met **SCALPED GHOST**.

Once they've passed, you head around the corner and down a few steps into a lounge area. But before you can explore anything else, the entire office converges, then enters the conference room — there's a meeting! Turn to **225**.

139

'You know, he tells everyone that he got a first in a Computer Science and Maths degree; well, I found out that he only got a Higher National Diploma, and he had to retake the exams because he failed the first time!'

'That does not surprise me. I mean, he tries to make up the gaps, I'll give him that, but he just doesn't have the grounding.'

'Anyhow, if your start-up takes off, then maybe Adam will have his chance to be Team Lead. How's it going?'

Hannah seems unaware of Theo's reaction, but you are hovering directly in front of him and see the colour drain from his face. A tight, nervous swallow and then he says as nonchalantly as possible, 'How did you know about that?'

'Oooh, was it top secret?' she laughs. 'I can't remember who it was that told me. Anyhow, is it not going well?'

'No, it's folded now. My friend, Danesh, it all got too much for him and… well, that's it.'

In a decisive move, he chucks the remaining water down his throat, says, 'See you later,' then heads towards the toilets. Hannah watches him, wondering what she'd done to upset him — start-ups fail every day; surely, he knew that…

That was a bit weird, but maybe you know already know something that can explain Theo's reaction. If you have ticked CLUE 12, turn to **31**. If not, you decide to continue while you're on a roll.

Turn to **213**.

140

You shrug apologetically and offer to help him search, but he dismisses you with a weak wave of the hand.

'Go away. You've taken up too much of my time already.'

However, when you start to head back to the workers' room, he stands up again, bellowing in his wheezy fashion.

'Not that way! You'll disturb everyone. I don't know what they do, but they're busy and that's the main thing. Being busy!'

He opens up another door, shoves you through it, then slams it shut. As in a dream, you find yourself back in the narrow corridor. The door has now vanished, replaced by the exposed brick wall. That was an interesting digression, but did it get you any closer to finding out who had the opportunity to give you the Thai curry? No, it did not!

You will have to accept that you've failed miserably at this part of the investigation and must tick the codeword **OPPORTUNITY**:

Now, if you want to investigate the "means" of your own murder, turn to **71**, but if you've already ticked the codeword MEANS, then it's time to focus on the motive! Turn to **246**.

141

Someone here deliberately gave you a massive dose of paracetamol, but how? And why? You feel a frisson of excitement, despite it being about your own murder. At least it's something interesting to do, instead of watching Hannah produce a PowerPoint presentation detailing her glories.

However, the evening and night pass in the blink of an eye, and the next thing you know, Louisa is gathering the staff into the conference room to make an announcement.

'And so, this morning, we are going to take part in a Team-Bonding workshop. Head office thinks it will really boost our synergy!'

You spot many eye rolls, but no one dares to openly criticise. Indeed, they plaster on fake smiles as Louisa hands out the bingo cards. She — it has to be said — is not taking part. Apparently, the boss doesn't need to bond with anyone…

'You'll see statements on the card and you need to talk to each other to find the person who matches each statement. First one to find all of them is the winner, but you only have 5 minutes!'

Robert gives a chuckling 'boo' that everyone, including Louisa, ignores.

'Trying too hard, Robert,' you murmur. 'No one likes a toady!'

This is probably going to be a devastatingly boring morning, but the question is: Who do you want to oversee as they do the Team Bonding Bingo?

Robert	Turn to **182**
Hannah	Turn to **3**
Theo	Turn to **223**
Marta	Turn to **112**
Adam	Turn to **119**
Jan	Turn to **282**

142

It's a tight squeeze as the chair is, understandably, standing close to the conference table and you can't shift it back, but your stomach simply protrudes into the furniture, which is a handy trick!

You are sitting between Adam and Theo, and although Adam starts to shiver and look around nervously — 'Is there a window open?' he mumbles — Theo is now engrossed in an Instagram notification. You take a peek at his phone and see a memorial reel for Danesh. Is that a friend of Theo? It's the usual montage of photos showing Danesh in happy times but ends with the Samaritans number. The obvious conclusion is that he took his own life. Being nosy, you can't help wondering what his problems were and how he did it, but such morbid curiosities will have to wait. Louisa is rapping the table to get everyone's attention. Turn to **209**.

143

If you weren't already dead, the waiting would've killed you! Robert is the last one to arrive and complains about the traffic, much to everyone's obvious annoyance. Once he has a cup of coffee and is finally settled at his desk, you waft over and plan your next move. How are you going to find out what he overheard on that fateful day?

If you have met SCALPED GHOST, you should talk to her ***straight away*** (turn to **189**).

If not, you could send Robert a message, but only if you've ticked the codeword OUIJA (turn to **65**).

If you have neither of those choices, turn to **244**.

144

Right then, back to the drawing board! Motive seems a bit complicated and how does a ghost investigate that anyway? Surely, means and opportunity are simpler. That way you can eliminate the ones who are definitely innocent, then focus on the motives of the remaining suspects. It's a good plan, but which will you do first? Check out who has the burgundy Tupperware and cooks Thai cuisine (means) or who was in the office on the fateful day and could have brought you the curry (opportunity)?

Means Turn to **71**
Opportunity Turn to **88**

145

Trying to act like he has a very important role, Robert spots the wrongly delivered letter, tuts, then marches to the door. You glide after him, down the steep stairs, around the corner and into the offices below. The layout is similar but with a brand colour scheme of chocolate brown and teal, and promotional posters of happy, smiling people. It's really not clear what their business is — something to do with dentistry, perhaps? — but then again, you still don't remember what your own company does! Robert strides around to the equivalent of his own office and drops the letter onto a desk.

'Here you are, Miriam. Another one! Where do they get these postal workers from, eh?'

Miriam blinks myopically at him for a few seconds, then gestures for him to come closer. Blimey, is he having a fling with Miriam?

'Did you get it sorted out?'

Robert coughs nervously and looks around, but the office is otherwise empty.

'They're on their lunch.' Miriam reassures him. 'The missing Thunderbolt cables? Did you find them or find out what happened to them? Did Louisa say anything?'

He actually steps back under the barrage of questions, then laughs with fake bravado.

'Oh that. It's… dealt with.' He seems to realise what a weak, non-answer this is but tries to bluster his way out of it.

'Louisa trusts me implicitly. There's no problem. Anyway, must dash. Bye.'

Both you and Miriam stare at his rapidly departing back, then she settles back into her ergonomic chair before murmuring, 'Fudging the numbers to cover up a mistake. Well, we've all done that!'

Any information could be useful, although you're not sure whether Robert's poor stock-taking skills fall into that category. But just then, you notice something else. A slightly ajar door…

It's probably nothing, but while you're here, you might as well check it out. Turn to **206**.

146

Well, he was frustrated with Louisa's unwillingness to see his genius, and maybe he thought that Louisa would mistake his poisoned curry for her own lunch, seeing as they have the same Tupperware… No, that's unfeasible — if she did grab the 'wrong' lunch, she would have returned it straight away!

Add 5 PURGATORY points, then turn to **195**.

147

However, there is no need for another drop of ectoplasm — the storeroom door is already ajar. You slide through the gap and see Marta rummaging through the neatly stocked items. She grabs some pens, but to your shock, she then takes a toner cartridge and secretes it under her cardigan. She's a sneaky thief! Tick **CLUE 2**. And then with her ill-gotten gains, she leaves. You decide to stay and have a root around, but there is nothing of interest here. Not unless you like paperclips…

With a quick ooze, you open the door and exit the storeroom. Turn to **277**.

148

It's a desperate move, but you are all out of ideas. With the force of your anger, you actually descend right through the floor — that's a neat trick! — all the way down until you arrive back in the basement. There's just a moment of hesitation before you open the service door. Well, what's the worst thing that can happen? At first, there is nothing; the tunnel is empty, but then there is a faraway surge. It's as if your energy is calling to them. Calling to the mutants!

They erupt in a mass of distorted bodies and grotesquely enlarged heads, but you manage to spot the one that rushed at you before and beckon it in.

It could all end here if this thing attacks, but you gasp with relief as it hurtles past, then up the stairs.

You shout Adam's name, hoping that is enough of a command. Seconds later, you know it was.

His scream — pure concentrated terror — echoes around the building, but when you finally reach the vaulted office (going the conventional way, as your floor-traversing power seems to have vanished!), both the mutant and Adam have gone. Disappeared but not before confessing to his crime. Yes, the others are standing around with shocked and excited expressions — this is possibly the most dramatic day they've ever had in this office! And seeing as they've just been made redundant, that's saying something!

'It was him!'

'I can't believe it. Well, I mean, I can, he was a bit weird, wasn't he?'

And he thought that people would think Theo took his own life because his friend did.'

'What a nutter!'

'Poor Ashley!'

The police are called, but no one can explain where Adam went, only that he suddenly wasn't there anymore. And nobody mentions the mutant…

But you have justice! Adam is named as the man who murdered you. However, before you feel too triumphant about that, it should be noted that you are *still* haunting the now-empty offices. Maybe there is another factor that determines whether you move on or not. Maybe you should check out your PURGATORY point score. Turn to **45**.

149

You hold your finger out and wait for the ectoplasm to start dripping, but nothing! The green algae that's still coated over your hands must be blocking it! Damn! There's nothing you can do but wait outside the storeroom.

You can faintly hear Marta talking — she must be on her phone — and after ten minutes, she exits, goes back to her desk! Oh well.

You can now check out Hannah (turn to **37**), but if you've already done that, then turn to **13**.

150

If your PURGATORY point score is at 40 or higher, then turn **immediately** to **240**.

If your PURGATORY point score is below 40, then wrack your brains, weigh up all the evidence and decide again on your suspect. Who brought the paracetamol-laced Thai curry into the office?

Robert	Turn to **2**
Louisa	Turn to **235**
Marta	Turn to **165**
Jan	Turn to **229**
Adam	Turn to **61**
Theo	Turn to **272**

151

When you arrive, Hannah is writing an email with the signature '*Hannah Marshall, Marketing Lead*'. Like a slap in the face, the memory is there — the application, the interview, the success! And how annoyed she was! Tick **CLUE 1**.

It was you who got the job, not Hannah, but you suppose it's fair enough that she has now got the promotion. Who else would it go to?

Hannah then minimises her browser screen to view her desktop, so you nose through her files and folders. Your head is practically on top of her shoulder, and she suddenly gives a shudder and looks in your direction. You freeze — can she sense you? — but then Hannah flaps a hand and mutters, 'Bloody fly!' You sigh with relief, then turn back to the screen, which is when you spot the folder labelled 'EVIDENCE'. Oh, that's intriguing! Evidence of what? Does Hannah suspect someone in the office of criminal behaviour? If only you could get her to click on it so you could read the files inside…

Tick **CLUE 4**.

At that moment, her phone pings, and she looks at the message notification, then says, 'Hmm, I'll call *you* later.'

After a minute of mulling over that prospect, she wanders off to the kitchen to grab a green Tupperware container from the fridge. Time has flown and, apparently, it's lunchtime. Turn to **220**.

152

She has a huge beehive hairdo and is wearing a brown dress. She looks friendly enough but is startled when she sees you.

'Oh, are you new here? Yes… I remember seeing you, I think. Didn't you have a cold?'

'It's a long story,' you reply, watching as she floats around Adam's desk, humming a song, and despite it being an old song, there's a chance that you recognise it…

If you managed to find a vinyl record, turn to **262**, but if you haven't, turn to **14**.

153

It's not like the shoes came with any instructions, so you're not sure what to expect. They fit you perfectly — presumably, phantom shoes fit everyone's feet — and then you wait until Robert is alone. The clock ticks past 5 PM, and Theo leaves first, then Adam, with an obvious sense of superiority. Once the door closes, you grab the WLAN again and send a most threatening message — `I will haunt you till your dying breath. Who gave me the curry?` — and start to march up and down the office.

The effect is instant. Robert gasps and looks around wide-eyed, hoping for a rational explanation, but the clacking of your heels continues up and down the floorboards. With all this energy, you weirdly start to manifest a smell too. The aroma of Thai curry fills the air and it's all too much for Robert.

'Ashley, don't hurt me!' He wails. 'I'm sorry what happened to you, but it wasn't me. I swear it wasn't me, but I did hear who gave you the curry. It was Hannah. Not me. It was Hannah! She said it was a get-well-soon gift from Louisa. But then you died. I didn't say anything, though, because I didn't want Louisa to get in trouble, but it wasn't her. I'm sure it wasn't her. I think Hannah lied. I'm sorry!' He's becoming quite hysterical now, but it sounded like the truth. Hannah gave you the poisoned curry!

If you have already discovered the TRUTH about Robert, turn to **266**. If not, turn to **75**.

154

You hold out a finger on your left hand, then watch with a mixture of fascination and disgust as the white mucus oozes out, before dripping onto the door handle. And with a click, the door opens! It's a success, no doubt, but when push comes to shove, it's still just a storeroom. The shelves are stacked full of well-organised office items, like pens and photocopier paper and— What's *that* doing here?

You crouch down to peer at the **rubber duck** which is sitting in the middle of the room.

Being a small space, you cannot get out of the way when the door swings open and Marta enters.

You swirl uncontrollably but eventually gather yourself together. And just in the nick of time! You spot Marta ostensibly picking up a few pens but also secreting a toner cartridge under her cardigan. The sneaky thief! Tick **CLUE 2**. Meanwhile, the rubber duck has vanished, leaving behind no clue as to why it was there in the first place. Marta then heads back to her desk, and before the door slams shut, you exit the storeroom too.

You could now enter the server room (turn to **255**), but if you have already been in there, turn to **277**.

155

You're absolutely convinced that you know where the prize is and glide through the office until reaching the kitchen. Robert and Adam are both extremely competitive, so they arrive seconds afterwards. It's a tight squeeze and in trying to keep out of their way, your left leg is now in the refrigerator. But that doesn't stop your own triumph when Adam opens the microwave door and grabs the prize. It's only a chocolate bar — you'd think it was a gold nugget from the way he punches the air! — but strangely, he doesn't notice the weird writing in mayonnaise on the microwave door…

There's no time to wonder about it though, as Louisa is wrapping up the team bonding session. And not a moment too soon. She looks like she's going to spend her lunch break in the nearest wine bar! Everyone heads either to their desks or the toilet, and you end up floating aimlessly in the large, vaulted office. Turn to **214**.

156

Why would you think this? Louisa was always positive about Theo — his work was good, which made her look good. Enough said!
Add 15 PURGATORY points, then turn to **150**.

157

It's a distinct case of "when the cat's away, the mice will play" and Theo and Jan are drinking coffee and chatting on the company time, but when Jan asks an innocent question, the mood darkens.

'So, how's your start-up going? You'll be the next one out, I'm sure!'

'What? How do you know about that?' Theo tries to chuckle, but it sounds nervous.

'Not sure. "Data something", was it?'

'No, it was just an idea. I'm staying for now.'

'Maybe not for much longer. Revenue is not good here and hasn't been for ages; I can see the Americans pulling the plug!'

While they gossip about the possibility of the company closing, you watch Theo relax. The topic of his start-up is clearly out of bounds, so he changes the subject completely.

'So, why did you and Ashley break up?'

Now it's Jan's turn to look uncomfortable, but when he answers, it's not as bad as you were expecting.

'Just liked different things. She liked parties, I liked watching TV…'

And suddenly, you have a flashback to standing in your kitchen, hands on hips, moaning about staying in, while Jan complained how tired he was. Yes, it was a 'fun while it lasted but let's call it a day' break-up. No real aggro, no red flags at all.

For some reason, Jan being decent irritates you — probably all the pent-up frustration of being dead! If you've ticked the codeword MIASMA, turn to **224**. If you haven't, turn to **51**.

158

You stand there, stumped for a while, then decide that there's nothing more you can do.

Tick the codeword **OPPORTUNITY**:

If you haven't yet investigated the "means" of your own murder, then you should do it now (turn to **71**) and hopefully, you'll have more success, but if you've already ticked the codeword MEANS, it's time to focus on the motive! Turn to **246**.

159

Did you think that, as Louisa didn't like Jan, Robert was prepared to gallantly murder him! That's preposterous and not even vaguely close to the truth! **Add 15 PURGATORY** points, then turn to **150**.

160

But as you approach, you realise that she is staring at *you* — she can see you! Which is why you assume she is another ghost and poke her face, but your finger goes straight through.

'What are you doing? Are you new to the realm? It can be a shock to your ethereal spirit. This was your funeral, wasn't it?' she intones knowledgeably, so you presume that she's a medium.

'Yes, but I don't really know what happened.'

'I sense a troubled aura. A disturbance in the ether.' You roll your eyes but wait for her to finish this announcement. 'It was an accident. You were not meant to die. It wasn't for you.'

'What are you talking ab— Ooof!'

Suddenly, the tether snaps taut, and you are pulled off your feet and away. And in the blink of an eye, you are back in the office. Turn to **115**.

161

Even though your computer has already been cleaned and rebooted for the next unfortunate schmuck who works here, the memory is so vivid, it's like you're back at your desk. You can even feel the sticky TAB key...

Email was the obvious choice as the picture was an arrow pointing **in**to a **box** — an INBOX, you might say!

You scroll down, not really sure what you're looking for until you see it. The announcement email from Louisa after the interview. The interview for the promotion to Marketing Lead, which you got and Hannah didn't.

> From: Louisa Baker
>
> To: London Team
>
> Just wanted to share the good news 😄 Ashley is now our new Marketing Lead.
> She has such managerial skills that she can run a perfectly coordinated event, even in chaotic situations - like a brewery! 😊
> Congrats!

If you have ticked CLUE 9, turn to **57**, but if you missed that particular nugget, turn to **283**.

162

As soon as you, Marta and Jan are in their office, Marta slams the door and rounds on him.

'Jan. Do you really think it's sensible to go to your ex's funeral?'

She pronounces his name Yan; yes, of course, he's Polish. You remember that! Jan Zapalska. And apparently, you went out with him, which is Marta's concern too.

'It looks very dodgy, you know, like serial killers who offer to help search for missing people when they know exactly where they dumped the body.'

You gasp silently. Body? Did Jan murder you?

'I have an alibi for that day when they think it happened. You know I was out for the face-to-face.' Tick **CLUE 3**. Marta looks unconvinced and a small grin appears on Jan's lips. 'I'm just being respectful. Plus, I want to have the morning off. Is that so bad?'

Well, it is a bit, you think, although Marta is smiling conspiratorially, and to be honest, you'd probably go too, if you weren't the corpse!

It looks like he's preparing to leave soon, so you better be ready to go with him. Except you've watched enough films to know that ghosts can't escape from their place of haunting. Unless, that is, you've learnt a trick from Clara the maid…

If you haven't yet met the ghost called Clara, then you are going to have to abandon any thoughts of attending your own funeral and must turn to **233**.

But if you have, then turn to **Appendix A** (What's on the Desk?) at the back of the book and choose the item that is the solution to Clara's riddle. When you have made your selection and noted its associated number, **return here**.

You must now **ADD the number** to this section, then turn to the new section. If it begins with "It was the logical choice…", then you have chosen correctly, but if not, accept defeat and turn to **233**.

163

With your nose held and a swift blow, you concentrate on the reasons why Hannah might hate you enough to poison you. Suddenly, your ears pop, and the scene transforms.

It's you! And you're sitting at your desk, reading a message. Hannah isn't there, but judging by the way you look sneakily around, she's not gone far and you're definitely up to something!

The message is from Hannah and about a meeting that Louisa was going to set up but obviously didn't. Hannah is livid — "so annoyed", "incompetence" and "can't organise a **** in a brewery!" — but what you see next is much, much worse...

Seconds later, you've printed out a screenshot of the message and left it on Louisa's desk. You squirm as you watch yourself run back to your desk, smirk and mutter, 'That should see off the competition!' And then the scene fades. Tick **CLUE 9**.

Did you really do that? What a horrible person! And, more importantly, did Hannah know that you'd done it? That would be a bona fide motive for murder and if you have ticked CLUE 1, turn immediately to **17**. If not, continue reading.

While you're taking all this in, you float out of the office and can now check out Marta (turn to **217**), but if you've already done that, then turn to **13**.

164

Nope! While Theo was hiding a pretty big secret and may well have resorted to murder to keep it under wraps, he had nothing to worry about with you. You were unaware of DataFusion's dark and illegal machinations and Theo knew that.

Add 5 PURGATORY points, then turn to **150**.

165

You think that Marta brought in the poisoned curry. Is this because she's obviously got a criminal mind or just because she had the same type of burgundy Tupperware? Well, in any case, let's find out who you think her intended victim was?

You	Turn to **111**
Hannah	Turn to **16**
Jan	Turn to **86**
Adam	Turn to **265**
Louisa	Turn to **125**
Theo	Turn to **83**
Robert	Turn to **218**

166

At first, Theo just laughs but eventually denies everything. You picked the wrong person!

Although you're quite happy to continue with the bingo, too many people are moving around this small space, making both time and the surroundings shift and judder. By the time everything settles again, Louisa is announcing the next activity. Turn to **275**.

167

Feeling like an idiot, and even more so when Chain-Smoking Ghost suddenly appears and shouts, 'What are you doing, you idiot?', you block your nose and blow hard, thinking of that last day. There is a pop and suddenly, the scenery changes.

You are sitting in the conference room, laptop on the desk, sneezing, blowing your nose and waiting for the morning Scrum to begin. You look very ill and should've stayed at home, but you'd just got the promotion and wanted to prove yourself.

'Oh well, no point crying over spilt milk,' you whisper and watch as Louisa, Robert, Theo, Marta, Adam and Hannah enter and take their seats.

'Ah-ha, so Jan wasn't in.' And although this information is very useful — he didn't have the opportunity to give you the curry if he wasn't in the office — Hannah's expression is more interesting. She looks furious and, judging from the frequent side eyes, she's furious *with you*. Tick **CLUE 1**.

But then the scene fades and you are back on the landing, and no amount of blowing and nose holding makes the pop happen. Maybe you have to wait to let the pressure build up again…

You have succeeded in this part of the investigation, so tick the codeword **OPPORTUNITY**:

Now, if you want to investigate the "means" of your own murder, turn to **71**, but if you've already ticked the codeword MEANS, it's time to focus on the motive! Turn to **246**.

168

By the time you've dripped the ectoplasm on the handle and squeezed through the gap, Marta is already on her phone. She frowns at the opened door, shuts it again, then continues her conversation.

'Not a bit. She's happy when you're not here; you know, she was going on in Scrum about how good Brexit is. I can't remember how she even got onto it, but we all just rolled our eyes and she shut up. Well, yes, obviously not Robert, poor sap!'

This sounds like juicy gossip, and although it's not clear who's on the other end of the line, you've got the sneaking suspicion that it's Jan.

'Ha ha, that's right, and I think he's still got no idea about the Thunderbolt cables, so you-know-who hasn't said anything. Anyway, I better get back. See you tomorrow.' And with that, she exits the storeroom. If you have ticked CLUE 2, turn to **25**. If not, turn to **219**.

169

You manage to sneak through the gap before Justin closes the door. He has a worried look on his face.

'God, I'll be glad to get back home. If I never have to visit London again, it'll be too soon!'

Meredith looks tired — maybe the jetlag is getting to her — and asks him what's wrong. He perches on the edge of the conference table, tugs his trouser leg into position, then leans forward.

'It's Kelsey. You know how she was going on about London being full of ghosts. All the beheaded

kings and queens! Well, she's apparently just seen a horde of mutants rushing into the Underground!'
Meredith frowns. Mutants?

'I really can't afford to have Kelsey lose it. Tell her to get herself together. This is going to be hard enough without her having a psychotic break! We should've done this remotely, saved on the airfare and hotels.'

Justin still looks worried, but if Meredith doesn't care, then why should he. It's above his pay grade, that's for sure! Kelsey did seem certain about what she'd seen though…

At that point, the door opens and one of the assistants enters, muttering about game changers and drilling down. You have no idea what she's said, but Meredith and Justin do — they walk out into the lounge area with big, white-teeth-gleaming smiles.

With everyone now milling around, there's a chance that the ghosts can notify you of anything interesting happening in their favourite areas — but only if you've **already met** them!

NSFW Ghost	Turn to **241**
Charlie	Turn to **79**
Pale Ghost	Turn to **122**

But if they're not an option, then you should investigate what the COO's minion is up to.
Turn to **221**.

170

Charlie hangs around Marta and Jan's office and if they're celebrating, it must mean one thing — Jan got the job! You are genuinely pleased for him, despite the break-up, and you know that Jan had no reason to murder you and wasn't even in the office that day. Do you want to spend this opportunity confirming what you already know? If you want to hear Marta and Jan's celebration, turn to **106**, but if not, you can choose a different ghost to check-in with. Remember, though, you must have **previously met** them!

NSFW Ghost	Turn to **268**
Pale Ghost	Turn to **296**

And if neither of those spectres are an option, then you should check out the Conference Room (turn to **169**).

171

'Was' being the operative word because he has now gone. Not vanished like Seventies man — you can hear him nearby and it sounds like he's brewing some coffee — but nevertheless gone. What was he looking for and did he find it?

If you want to chase after him to see if you can answer that, turn to **24**. If you'd prefer to stay and examine the desk, turn to **215**.

172

A rough-handled ladle is wedged into a mass of stinking, rotten flesh. It heaves with the incessant wriggling of maggots and the stench almost makes you vomit, but undaunted, you scoop up a pile and hurl it into the moat. The reaction is instant! The creature bursts through the surface of the algae at a frightening speed, ferociously snapping for the food. But it's like no creature you've seen before…

As though four or five mannequins have been charred and melted into each other, it is monstrous chimera. In the second that it is clear of the algae, you glimpse a hand protruding from a thigh and two overlapping faces — both screaming 'Save me!' — on a shoulder. It is a blackened mass of suffering humanity, and you can only wonder what they did during their life on Earth for them to end up here in this moat! Sickened and disturbed, you must **add 20 PURGATORY** points, then head quickly towards the gap (turn to **187**).

173

'To be honest,' Beehive Ghost continues, 'You could be a piece of work when you were alive!' You'd like to deny it, but she has made a valid point. However, before you can say any more, there is a strangled cry. Beehive Ghost is starting to swirl around, getting brighter and brighter. She manages to shout, 'There was something else that happened that day, but… oh! This must be because Cilla made me so happy! Thank yooooooouuuuu…'

And the brown dress and ginormous hairdo become a thin vortex of white light before dissipating into nothing. Beehive Ghost has moved onto the next plane.

Subtract 10 PURGATORY points and **strike Beehive Ghost** from the Met-A-Ghost list.

If you have ticked the codeword LIMBO, you can attempt to revisit this time and try to discover what the ghost was talking about (turn to **78**). If not, you should carry on with your investigation into the motive for your murder.

So, who's next?

> Marta   Turn to **211**
> Hannah   Turn to **72**

But if you've already done that, then drift towards the landing to think about your strategy (turn to **63**).

174

Although Louisa looks strangely conflicted — as if she wants to say something but isn't sure how to say it — your mother's need to get this over with is stronger, so she snaps, 'Ashley's stuff?'

You desperately want to hug your mum and tell her that you're OK — a bit jaundiced but reconciled with it all — but Louisa then guides her to your old office where your remaining items have been packed up in a cardboard box. It's too painful to follow, so instead you go to see what's happening elsewhere.

If you've **already met** them, then you could see if the other ghosts have anything to report.

    Charlie   Turn to **79**
    Pale Ghost   Turn to **122**

But if they're not an option, then you should investigate what the COO's minion is up to.
Turn to **221**.

175

There is only Robert in the large, vaulted office. Well, Robert and the Beehive Ghost, who is poking her finger into the bacon stew that he is eating. Straight away, you spot the container.

'Hmm, glass Pyrex.'

'Class pirates? What are you talking about?' Beehive Ghost has, at least, stopped prodding the food.

'It's just a modern thing. Why are you sticking your fingers in the stew?'

'Oh, his wife throws all the leftovers together and this poor man has to eat them. I mean who would put bacon with tomato sauce and turnips?'

You have to agree — it does sound awful. But you want to know more about the other two men too.

'Oh, they go out. Sometimes, they're out all lunch; sometimes, they bring stuff back in with them. But not together. Never together. Why?'

Tick **CLUE 5**.

After you've explained about the paracetamol in the homemade curry, she floats purposefully upwards and over Robert's monitor to reach you.

'That's the stuff that killed Theo's friend. Topped himself, he did. Adam was ever so sympathetic, he was.'

'I'm surprised Theo told him. Like you say, they don't go out for lunch together, so it's not like they're good friends.'

Beehive Ghost nods. 'He didn't. It was that woman, the boss. Mentioned it in front of the whole office. Bit indiscreet, if you ask me, but I think she was trying to impress this one here that she was all caring.' She throws a look back towards Robert who has dutifully finished his strange and boring lunch and murmurs, 'I wonder if there's any chocolate around…' With the mention of the C-word, Beehive Ghost starts choking, clutching her throat and turning purple, before vanishing.

So, what should you do next? You could talk to:

> NSFW Ghost   Turn to **243**
> Charlie   Turn to **108**
> Party Ghost   Turn to **208**

…but only if you've **previously met** them!

And if you've finished with the spectres, then you could check out the kitchen for any clues (turn to **35**), but if you've already done that, then tick the codeword **MEANS** and think about the next stage of your investigation.

If you've ticked the codeword OPPORTUNITY, turn to **246**, if not, turn to **6**.

176

Without warning, your feet begin to rise, as though they're filled with helium! The rest of you flips upside down and you are unceremoniously dragged higher and higher, through the ceiling and into the attic. At which point, the phenomenon stops and you collapse at the feet of a Grey Lady Ghost. Long grey hair, long grey dress (which could have been from anytime between medieval and Victorian) and grey skin.

'Oh hello, I've never been up here before. Well, of course, I haven't, why would I?'

Stop babbling, you tell yourself, then ask, 'Why are you haunting this place?' Which could be considered a very insensitive question if the poor woman has been murdered here…

Luckily, she just shrugs.

''I'm a generic ghost. People everywhere, in every time, have always seen Grey Lady Ghosts. It's a combination of poor lighting, poor eyesight and alcohol! When one has been imagined so many times, one tends to be brought into existence.'

Well, that's unexpected! And for a few seconds, you are speechless, but eventually ask, 'And did you make me come up here? Why?'

'You have my opera glasses and I'm expected at the Marylebone Theatre soon for a stint of haunting there. Grey Lady Ghosts and theatres are a classic combination.'

Fair enough, and you hand the glasses over. The Grey Lady turns to leave, then pauses and says, 'You're the latest one, aren't you? I know that you shouldn't have died. The intended victim was a man. Does that help?'

But without waiting for a reply, she disappears, and you gently sink through the rafters and back into the office. Turn to **43**.

177

They are, indeed, steep stairs with polished wooden treads that any Health and Safety officer would curse, but you make it to the bottom without having flashbacks to an untimely tumble.

'Nope. Didn't break my neck here,' you mutter, darting out of the way when a woman — Miriam, according to her ID badge — pushes the main door open and enters. Before the door closes again, you go through the gap, find yourself on a station concourse and announce: 'Marylebone Station, as I live and breathe!' even though none of that is true. There are numerous ghosts mingling with the commuters, and all look like they'd rather be anywhere else than here. You take another step forward, intending to chat with the man who has a piece of scaffolding protruding from his chest — that must have hurt! — but a sudden blast of air explodes, sending you flying back into the office. You collapse in a crumpled heap at the bottom of the stairs.

'You can't leave. Did you not know that? Actually, that's not exactly true, but it's tricky. By the way, I'm Clara.'

Still feeling shook up, you raise your eyes to see a young woman with her head resting on a shoulder, her neck bent literally at a right angle. She is quite a sight!

'So, I'm destined to haunt *only* the office? That's just great!'

'Something must have happened here. I mean, look at me. I broke my neck back in 1910 because of them blooming stairs, and I think I'm here for as long as the stairs are.'

Which, seeing as they're Grade II listed, is probably a very long time, but you sensitively don't tell Clara that.

'Does that mean I can't visit my family?' but as soon as you ask the question, you realise that you actually can't remember them.

'Some ghosts have left if it's a way to discover how they died.'

You perk up with this news; that might be useful.

'It's all about escaping, isn't it? And in order to **escape**, you need to solve the riddle…'

And Clara wedges her wobbling head up, so she can whisper in your ear. Turn to **290**.

178

It's an interesting side to Louisa that you've never seen before. She is shovelling biscuits into her mouth and doomscrolling through LinkedIn posts. It's another professional woman's newsfeed — Astrid Pomeroy — and Louisa is forensically examining each and every post. Soon, she pauses, takes a deep breath and mutters, 'I knew it!'

Knew what? You lean in and take a closer look.

> No place for negativity! I once worked with someone who was racist - there's no other word to describe it.
> I was scared about the consequences and possible victimisation, but sometimes you have to stand up for what is right. So I reported the person, and they had to leave their post.
> It might not be easy, but the right thing is always the best thing!
>
> Astrid Pomeroy | 2:57 PM

If you have found CLUE 6, turn to **48**. If you have not, turn to **121**.

179

No, Jan and Adam's orbits rarely intersected — they were not friends but also not enemies. There was no reason at all for Adam to want Jan dead.
Add 15 PURGATORY points, then turn to **195**.

180

Hannah goes into a mild trance, then opens the EVIDENCE folder. There's only one document in it — her investigation is going as well as yours! — and with an extra burst of concentration and a squeaky phantom fart, you make her click on the file. Head to **Appendix D** (The 'Evidence' File) at the back of the book but remember **this section number**, as you will return here afterwards.

You stare at the screen, frantically trying to make sense of it but the facts are undeniable. Hannah is also investigating who gave you the burgundy Tupperware, but why? And what does it mean that Adam, Marta or Louisa had that type? At this point, Hannah gives an irritated shake of her head, then closes the folder, saying, 'Now, where was I?'

Does it really rule the others out, though? Could someone be trying to frame a colleague? Could one of them have borrowed burgundy Tupperware from someone else? Oh, so many unanswered questions!

Hannah is now on the phone, talking about SEOs, but have you finished with her? If you've recently ticked the codeword LIMBO and want to try out this new skill, turn to **120**.

If not, then you give up on Hannah and can now check out Adam (turn to **278**) or Marta (turn to **211**). And if you've already done that, then drift to the landing to think about your strategy (turn to **63**).

181

'Hallo there. You look a bit yellow! I'm Clara.'

Well, she seems friendly enough, although that dig about your jaundice hurts. Too soon, Clara! And while you're thinking of something to say, your eyes drift to the concourse outside the offices. You must have a wistful expression because Clara nudges your arm and says, 'Most new ghosts want to leave their haunting place, but it's tricky. There is a way to escape though; you just need to identify this object.' And then Clara hands you a small scrap of paper.

> Tickling the ivories may hint at the truth, while shifting control will give absolute proof.

If you think you know the object that is the answer to the puzzle, turn quickly to **Appendix A** (What's on the Desk?) at the back of the book and find the number associated with that object. But remember you need to return to 181 afterwards!

In the future, if you are given the chance to **ESCAPE**, you must **add** the object's number to the section number.

While you are processing all that information, Clara has vanished, so you head on up to the landing. Turn to **287**.

182

You peer over his shoulder, making a red flush bloom on his cheek, and read the first statement.

Loves Asian cuisine

You and Robert both clack your teeth as you weigh up the possibilities. Who do you think Robert should talk to first? Who do you think is the food lover?

Hannah	Turn to **27**
Adam	Turn to **69**
Jan	Turn to **239**
Marta	Turn to **281**
Theo	Turn to **166**

183

He snatches them from your hand, lights one, then smiles a broad grin of utter pleasure…

Until the lung-hacking cough erupts, making him collapse against the banister. You realise, though, that he's weeping too, with an expression of abject disappointment on his face. As he wipes the tears across his cheek, he mumbles, 'Thought that might do it. Might be my turn to go,' but then bows his head. It's an awkward silence, so when he's recovered a little, you remind him about the memory.

'Oh yes, well, the one they call Robert. He was in this small cubicle — doing what I do not know — but he looked cagey and then he heard something from your office. I didn't hear it, but he was snooping good and proper! Later on, after you'd died but before you turned up here, the coppers were round asking about food and poison and he went as white as a ghost. Not that we're white, but you know what I mean.'

'So, you think he heard whoever gave me the Thai curry in the Tupperware?'

Chain-Smoking Ghost looks confused and mutters, 'Food? Made with ties? Like from suits?' but you ignore him and carry on regardless.

'Why didn't he say what he heard? WHO IS HE PROTECTING?'

This last part is practically shouted, but the dramatic effect is lost, as Chain-Smoking Ghost has vanished, then so do you. When you next reappear, the offices are empty, although the station concourse is packed. From this, you conclude it's Saturday, so wait for the work week to start again, and when it does, you stake out Robert's office until he arrives. Turn to **143**.

184

Maybe you didn't notice it at first or maybe other strange phenomena are at work, but you realise there is a glass on the floor between two tables. It has a wedge of pineapple on the rim and a straw, which you attempt to slurp through but can't. Still, you recognise the smell and shake your head. Why is there a **pina colada** in the work lounge? No one living has noticed it, so it must be spectral…

'Weird things happen all the time.'

You jolt up, gasping in anticipation of the smack of your head against the nearest table, but, of course, you simply pass straight through it.

'Ooh, that made me wince! Mind you, anything that reminds me of being bashed in the head sends a shiver through me.'

You look over at the pale ghost, who's currently examining the water cooler, and hazard a guess that she's from the 1940s. However, when you tactfully ask if she died during a bombing, she laughs.

'No, no, this station escaped relatively unscathed. I died from carbon monoxide poisoning. It was cold; some numbskull brought in a brazier and a couple of hours later, we all had a headache and that's the last thing I remember. Don't know why the others aren't here, though. No, I mention the head bashing because of that woman who fell out of the window during a party. They were all dancing and singing to someone they called Emcee Hammer and didn't even notice she'd gone. You had to laugh, though. Once she'd died, she came right back in and carried on singing — "You can't touch this!" The modern music is quite stupid, isn't it?'

You refrain from pointing out that the song is over three decades old and instead, nod in agreement.

By now, the living workers have finished their lunch and are heading back to their offices, but the pina colada and pale ghost remain. She points at the cocktail.

'That must mean something, else it wouldn't be here, and I happen to know for a fact that you drank pina coladas at the office summer party.'

A vision of you swam before your eyes. You were talking too loudly, laughing too much and eventually, had to be taken home in a taxi.

'But there was someone who wouldn't touch a pina colada…' Tick **CLUE 7**.

Record that you have met **PALE GHOST** and if you want to quiz her about this mysterious statement, you're too late — she's gone! — so you must decide how to fill the rest of the afternoon. Turn to **115**.

The journey goes by in a blur, and you wonder about the wisdom of this escape. However, when you arrive at the field, you feel yourself take shape again and can take in the surroundings. A field? There is a group of mourners nearby, who are receiving the visitors. Ah-ha, they must be your family, so you drift closer to check them out. Nothing! No memories, no connection, nada! But you assume they are your parents and sister and then you overhear your mother say, 'This is all modern, John. Why not a cremation instead of being in a field?'

'She wouldn't have wanted anything in a church,' your father replies. 'And you know it's better to bury her. Even though they've done the post-mortem, if they find who did this, they might need to…' And although he makes a shovelling gesture with his hands, he can't quite say 'dig her up' and starts to cry. You feel a twinge of sadness for his obvious pain, but it's dulled by not remembering the poor man at all.

'The police haven't said for sure that someone did do it,' your mum says as she hugs him.

'There's no other explanation. She didn't do it deliberately and it wasn't an accident. My daughter is not stupid!'

Poignant how he's still referring to you in the present tense, you think, not accepting that his daughter has gone. Or not, as the case is…

With your next glance around, you realise that the coffin is already positioned over the open grave — the ceremony must be starting soon — meanwhile, the undertakers are standing next to the hearse, looking appropriately solemn. It's not clear just how long this tether is, but it's worth testing its limitations. So, what would you like to do? Investigate inside your own coffin (turn to **47**) or eavesdrop on the undertakers (turn to **207**)?

186

At first, you are confused. Normally, when you look out of a window, you see the outside — surely the afterlife isn't so different! — but this is a station concourse…

With a flash, the memory pops into your head. It's London. Marylebone Station to be precise. You lived in London, and the offices where you worked were in the station building itself. How on Earth could I afford that, you wonder, as you watch the people below. A never-ending stream of bodies heading to or from the platforms, but then you realise that some have stopped and are staring up at you. A cyclist with a dented, blood-stained helmet, a woman wearing a long, old-fashioned skirt which is torn, revealing her amputated leg, a young man with a blade protruding from the front of his tracksuit top. And between them all, a fluttering, untethered, **American-style police tape**. Why on Earth is that there?

POLICE LINE DO NOT CROSS POLICE LINE DO NOT CROSS

As you watch, more and more stop. The dead of the station, you presume and feel decidedly depressed.

'Why haven't they moved on?' you snap, before remembering that no one can hear you anymore. You step away from the window and, for a second, hope to catch your own reflection, but no. You're invisible as well as silent.

It's probably best not to dwell on that, so you focus on your investigation. However, a strange swirling in the atmosphere is verging on tornado strength, so you decide that a change of scenery is needed and leave the office (turn to **64**).

187

You step into another huge room, but this one is so vast you can't see the end. It's just full of office cubicles. There are hundreds and each one has someone at their desk, busily working on something. But then you notice the young people at the side of the room, looking eager to please and prove their worth. Are they the interns? Do you want to try to speak with any of the cubicle workers (turn to **81**) or head over to chat with an intern (turn to **249**)?

188

So, it turns out that being dead is a bit like working in the office. You will get regular appraisals and quarterly reviews in which you have to demonstrate your worth, and hopefully, you might get the promotion you desire. But for now, you'll just have to keep your nose to the grindstone and show how passionate you are about haunting. Surely, eternity can't be that long…

Your game ends here!

189

It takes a couple of circuits around the landing, plus a 'Yoo-hoo!' until Scalped Ghost appears. She looks a bit peeved by the disturbance, but when you explain that Robert had overheard you being given the poisoned food, she pats your arm sympathetically.

'Do you know, I do believe I remember that. He looked awful worried, sat in that small box, talking to that hand-phone. He was saying, "I've messed up the order. You must change it. My boss will kill me!" And then he sat there, staring into space for ages, but suddenly, he looked towards your old office — proper interested at first, then he frowned and muttered, "What? That doesn't sound like Louisa! She wouldn't gift food to anyone. She doesn't even like Thai food. And especially not to my wife's friend. She wouldn't risk what we have together!" That's all I remember. Does it help?'

You nod slowly, but before you can thank Scalped Ghost, she hands you a **gold ribbon**, saying, 'I have no use for this, but it complements your skin,' then disappears.

You meander back to the vaulted office, and if you have ticked the codeword OUIJA, you can now turn to **65**. If not, turn to **244**.

190

Marta is obviously an office thief — she must have been talking to her 'fence' or whoever it is that takes the stolen goods! — but was she worried that you knew about her criminal secret? It could be a motive, but did you hear that she used the present tense in the statement "the other one that could cause trouble *is being* dealt with"? Seeing as you're dead, you can't be 'the other one'!

And that means, Marta would have no reason to murder you. This is progress, indeed, but it would be good to know who the mystery person is too. If you have ticked CLUE 11, turn to **234**, but remember **this section number** because you will have to return here afterwards!

And with that revelation, Marta exits the storeroom. Although you're still deep in thought, you've got enough wits left to notice the packet of cigarettes on the shelf opposite. That's unusual, so you give it a poke and to your amazement, your finger doesn't go straight through — the packet moves! That's got to be useful, so you grab the **spectral cigarettes**, wait for the ectoplasm to build up again, then leave.

Marta is back at her desk, so you could now check out Hannah (turn to **37**), but if you've already done that, then turn to **13**.

191

After a few minutes, the cacophony stops, then Louisa walks into the kitchen and retrieves the — (cue drumroll) — burgundy Tupperware! Well, that is definitely something worth noting! Much later, and with an air of great importance and busy-ness, Hannah grabs the green Tupperware.

Once the kitchen is cleared out, you head to the lounge area to see if you can discover what the noise was, but other than a lingering smell of charred flesh, there is nothing untoward. Now is probably a good time to interrogate the other ghosts (turn to **55**).

192

But there is no one left in the lounge area — this interview is the last one, so Theo has wandered off. You spot him standing in the kitchen, eating a crunchy muesli yoghurt — isn't that Jan's? Tick **CLUE 10**.

You can't help thinking that this petty food thievery is not helping you solve the mystery of your murder, so it's time to check on the other people still in the office. But who do you want to interrogate in your ghostly fashion?

Adam	Turn to **278**
Hannah	Turn to **72**
Marta	Turn to **211**.

193

'Well,' and he leans closer, conspiratorially. 'There is a phantom office, where the Workaholic Ghost is, but don't feed the thing in the swampy moat! To access the office, you need ectoplasm to open the door, so just hold your finger out and the white fluid will drip off onto the handle. It's easy!'

Tick the codeword **ECTOPLASM** if you haven't done so yet, but when you try to ask him about the location of these mysterious offices, he's gone!

As you're down here, it would make sense to have a look around, but do you want to check out the rest of the bicycle section (turn to **26**) or the nearby boiler room (turn to **131**)?

194

With a sardonic curl of the lip, Marta leans forward, quietly utters an expletive, then goes to talk to someone else. She was NOT the right choice!

Although you're quite happy to continue with the bingo, too many people are moving around this small space, making both time and the surroundings shift and judder. By the time everything settles again, Louisa is announcing the next activity. Turn to **275**.

195

If your PURGATORY point score is at 40 or higher, then turn immediately to **240**.

If your PURGATORY point score is below 40, then wrack your brains, weigh up all the evidence and decide again.

What was Adam's plan? How did he think the poisoned curry was going to get from the fridge and into his victim? What would he gain from the murder? And, most important of all, who was the intended victim?

You	Turn to **114**
Hannah	Turn to **276**
Jan	Turn to **179**
Robert	Turn to **46**
Louisa	Turn to **146**
Theo	Turn to **210**
Marta	Turn to **263**

196

You're not 100% sure, but the evidence suggests that Jan has been sneaking off for job interviews, while Marta covers for him. Was he at one on the day you were given the Thai curry? Maybe, and perhaps this jaunt out is just another one…

Turn back to **67** to decide your next step.

197

After a few deep breaths, you nod, although you feel more confused than ever.

'I don't think you'd risk spending the rest of your life in prison when you could've just got another job. Your career was everything to you. But why would Louisa put paracetamol in her own curry?'

'I'm not sure now that it was Louisa's food. I was doing some investigating after you died, in case someone did see me take the curry out of the fridge, and she wasn't the only one with the burgundy Tupperware. So, I have no idea who brought the curry in and why it was poisoned! But I promise you, I just gave you the curry, thinking that Louisa would miss her food, realise that you'd taken it and be cross with you. Payback for the interview sabotage! Are you there?'

It takes a moment for her words to register and then you realise that, with your temper calming, you have become your usual invisible ghost self again. Still, you can at least cross Hannah off your suspect list — she might have given you the curry, but she didn't poison it. It seems that you were an inadvertent victim in someone else's vendetta!

You half expect the shimmering bright light to come for you as it did Clara, but there's nothing. Maybe you've still got work to do before justice can be delivered! However, as you hover, feeling somewhat bereft, you feel a strange sensation in your feet…

This may seem like an odd question, but do you have a pair of vintage opera glasses? If you do, turn to **54**, but if not — and let's face it, why would you have opera glasses? — then you're probably just imagining things. It's been a long day!

Turn to **257**.

198

It was the logical choice — there is literally an ESC key on it! Make a note that when you are given an opportunity to **ESCAPE** from the office, you must **add 65** to the section you are at.

However, the ESC key needs to be pressed and that's a bit more difficult. Three times you watch your entire hand sink through the keyboard and desk before wondering whether there's a way to make Louisa press it. Aiming for a telepathic connection, you concentrate very hard. With your non-existent breath being held and furrowed brow, you simply look as though you're straining to go to the toilet, so it should come as no surprise when a spectral fart comes out. It's a tiny, odourless 'parp', but Louisa suddenly looks around, mutters, 'What the…?' and inexplicably presses the ESC key. The ability to make the living do what you want is a useful, albeit short-lived, skill to have, so ignore the embarrassment and tick the codeword **MIASMA**.

You now feel an unpleasant pull on your intestines — or, at least, where your intestines used to be. Is this just the aftermath of your gas or did it work? Louisa then stands up, straightens her skirt and exits the office. Like a balloon tethered to a child, you bob along after her. It worked! Turn to **185**.

199

Shouting, 'Follow me, I'll explain on the way,' you hurtle back down to the cupboard and use the magical key to fling open the door. Conscripted Ghost gazes upon his mortal remains, his eyes welling up with fondness and regret.

'Of course, in those days, it was a sin to take your own life, so it looks like some kindly folks hid me in here to save my family of the shame.'

Unsurprisingly, you see him start to fade and swirl — if this doesn't get a ghost to move on, you don't know what would!

Just before the brightness becomes too intense, he shouts, 'I've just remembered. You weren't the

target. He was trying to kill someone else! Good byeeeeee.' And then he is gone.
Subtract 10 PURGATORY points.
You are concerned that the window of opportunity for finding your killer is closing fast. After all, you can't investigate an empty office, but Conscripted Ghost has given you a highly important clue, so perhaps you have learnt all you need to know. It's time to put your money where your mouth is!
Turn to **127**.

200

You did find out a lot and you definitely have some suspicions, but there's nothing concrete! And as is so often the case, time passes, people change jobs and there are no more clues to get, because everyone has forgotten the strange case of the poisoned office worker.

The days pass by, fellow ghosts come and go, and at one point you hear that mushrooms have become the dominant species on Earth! But you've only been dead a month or so, haven't you? Time is, indeed, a bit strange here. Maybe you can go back a little and try to make more progress in your detective work.

You can keep the acquired clues, objects, codewords and ghosts — just **add 30 PURGATORY** points and turn to **213**.

201

A slight vibration of energy starts to move your molecules around. Is it happening? Have you done enough?

The answer to that is apparently, 'no', as you remain in your ghostly form. Disappointed, you head to your old office, and as you stare at your old desk, a tiny idea begins to unfold in your mind.

'Really? Could it be as simple as that?' you mumble. Moving on to the next realm is always described as 'going towards the _____.' Maybe if you take that instruction literally, it might work.

Turn to **Appendix A** (What's on the Desk?) at the back of the book and pick the item on your desk that best fits the gap. Make a note of its associated number, then **return here**.

Add the object's number to this section, then turn immediately to the new section.

202

Although Louisa looks strangely conflicted — as if she wants to say something but isn't sure how to say it — your mother's need to get this over with is stronger, so she snaps, 'Ashley's stuff?'

You desperately want to hug your mum and tell her that you're OK — a bit jaundiced but reconciled with it all — but Louisa then guides her to your old office where your remaining items have been packed up in a cardboard box. It's too painful to follow, so instead you go to the Conference Room — the 'fireside chat' is about to start! Turn to **104**.

203

But your plan is instantly thwarted by the closed door — you can't go through it! However, if you've ticked the codeword ECTOPLASM, turn to **154**.

If not, then you can't enter the storeroom, and unfortunately, the server room is also closed and therefore, out of bounds. You slump dejectedly and bored onto one of the comfy chairs. Turn to **40**.

204

There were no ill feelings or worries between these two. Louisa was happy that Theo did his job well enough, so she could reflect in his glory.

Add 15 PURGATORY points, then turn to **150**.

205

'It was a bouquet for my wife!' Robert snaps defensively.

To his credit, Adam simply reminds Robert that he hadn't said the flowers were for anyone else, which makes Robert turn an ugly purplish colour due to annoyance and embarrassment, before stomping off. Tick **CLUE 8**.

You then realise that Adam has written the number "**7**" on his card, which is weird, and although you're quite happy to continue with the bingo, too many people are moving around this small space, making both time and the surroundings shift and judder. By the time everything settles again, Louisa is announcing the next activity. Turn to **275**.

206

But the stairs tell you it's actually the basement! There is some light entering from grimy, small windows near the ceiling but otherwise, it is a dim, musty space filled mostly with bicycle stands. Naturally, the whole horror film setting would not be complete without a resident ghost, and this one would have chilled your blood if you had any.

'Hello! I don't get many ghost visitors down here,' he says, even though his entire lower jaw is missing. You grimace and garble an indecipherable greeting. He tries to wave a welcoming gesture, but every limb is broken, bent, twisted and ruptured, and it ends up being an uncoordinated spasm.

'I was asleep down in the tunnel. Probably had a bit too much to drink and woke up to go to the toilet. I was hit by a train. Luckily, it was slowing to come into the station, but it still catapulted me through the air. I must have died mid-trajectory because when I landed, I was in here, but my body was still out there in the service tunnel.'

When was this?'

'Not sure, but I remember everyone talking about the virus and lockdown.'

Aaah, yes, you remember the tale of the homeless man killed on the Underground line and how you'd dismissed it so casually at the time. You're not so nonchalant now, though, when the victim is standing in front of you with his mangled and torn body!

You quickly get over this shock and realise that Mangled Ghost may have seen some crucial evidence that can help you, but what do you want to ask him?

If you want to know whether he's seen any of the office workers down here, turn to **270**.

If you'd rather ask him about any useful ghostly skills or insider knowledge, then turn to **193**.

207

They are in the middle of a hushed conversation, which mostly consists of needing a cigarette and which pubs they'll be in this evening — lucky things! — but then one of them asks, 'That colour looked tricky to cover. How did you do it?'

'Bit of lilac concealer underneath the normal base,' he replies. 'Although I have heard that Alka Selzer in the embalming fluid also gets rid of jaundice. Never tried it though. Hold up, they're getting started now.'

As a loud, projected voice begins to proclaim your many attributes, you feel your tether tighten, bringing you back to the mourners. Who did you escape with?

> Adam   Turn to **103**
> Jan   Turn to **261**
> Louisa   Turn to **23**

208

No sooner have you arrived in the corridor between Jan and Marta's office and the toilets, then Party Ghost appears, doing the strange squat/scooting shuffle, before freezing to announce 'Stop! Hammer time!' She then falls over, cackling hysterically. It's got to be said — her afterlife looks like it's a nonstop laugh!

When she finally calms down, you ask if she's seen anything going on with food or Tupperware, seeing as she hangs around the kitchen. Party Ghost stares at the ceiling for a while, then jerks and points emphatically.

'Yes! Yes, there was something about Tupperware. One of the young men had this nice wine-coloured tub and the other one — you know, the one who's full of himself — he saw this and started joking about it. Saying that he copied the boss, trying to get into her good books. The one with the tub looked embarrassed and said it was just a coincidence, but he's never brought in any food since then. Does that help?'

You're not sure, but any information has to be good, doesn't it? However, Party Ghost has already danced away without waiting for your response. So, what should you do next?

You could now talk to:

>   NSFW Ghost   Turn to **243**
>   Beehive Ghost   Turn to **175**
>   Charlie   Turn to **108**

…but only if you've **previously met** them! And if you've finished with the spectres, then you could check out the kitchen for any clues (turn to **35**), but if you've already done that, then tick the codeword **MEANS** and think about the next stage of your investigation.

If you've ticked the codeword OPPORTUNITY, turn to **246**, if not, turn to **6**.

209

At this point, however, you are distracted by the splatter of blood which appears gradually on the wall above Louisa's left shoulder. From watching enough crime programmes, you feel confident enough to guess that it was a gunshot to the head, but where's the body? Who was the victim? There is no answer to that — only a small bunch of **daffodils** appear, hovering near the blood stain. Why daffodils?

You sigh impatiently with this obscure apparition, which makes the flowers fade away, and then you realise that Louisa is asking whether anyone wants to go to the funeral.

Hannah: 'I can't go. Seeing as I'm the only one in Marketing now, I have a lot to catch up on. Especially, since I've been promoted too.'

Jan: 'I think so. The police have already questioned me. Exes are the first to be suspected, aren't they? But I've got nothing to hide, so, yes, I'll go.'

Robert: 'I'll—' 'No, Robert,' interjects Louisa, 'I'm going. As Director, I have to make an appearance, so I need my Office Manager here, holding the fort.'

Marta: 'No.'

Adam: 'Yes, we were good friends. Of course, I want to pay my respects.'

Theo: 'No, not my thing, you know what I mean?'

The meeting wraps up after that, but you've definitely learnt quite a bit about your former colleagues! And now you have a decision to make — do you want to go to the funeral? If you'd rather stay in the office and avoid the queasiness of seeing your own coffin, turn to **233**. If you are intrigued by who attends your funeral and what they might say about you, then who will you accompany?

Louisa	Turn to **133**
Adam	Turn to **15**
Jan	Turn to **162**

210

You think that Adam wanted to murder Theo — but why? If you have ticked CLUE 5, turn to **38**. If not, turn to **254**.

211

But before you reach her office, you see Marta heading towards the storeroom and the door slams shut before you can get in. If you have ticked:

| ECTOPLASM | Turn to **168** |
| ECTOPLASM *and* CAUL | Turn to **274** |

If not, there's nothing you can do but wait outside the storeroom. You can faintly hear her talking — she must be on her phone — and after ten minutes, she exits and goes back to her desk! Oh well. You can now check out Adam (turn to **278**) or Hannah (turn to **72**). But if you've already done that, then drift towards the landing to think about your strategy (turn to **63**).

212

Adam is alone, having escaped the chattering noise in the lounge. He looks stunned too — no doubt wondering how bad a reference he might get — will Louisa mention the lies and complaining? You start marching up and down, the noise immediately reverberating around the room. Adam looks around, eyes darting into each corner and you can see him muttering, 'Who is it? What's going on?' His face is blanched. He looks scared to death. But you have no sympathy; indeed, your rage builds and builds, reaching a crescendo of cacophony. And it's not just the sound of your shoes clattering on the floor. You are also manifesting your voice.

'CONFESS! CONFESS! CONFESS!'

He clamps his hands over his ears and folds over onto his keyboard, crying, 'I'm sorry, Ashley, I'm so sorry. I didn't mean it.'

But you don't want his apology; you want him behind bars! However, your strategy isn't working! What else could you possibly do?

If you've ticked the codeword PREMONITION, turn to **148**. If you haven't, turn to **4**.

213

How to discover who had sufficient motive to want you dead? This question has kept you busy for hours, and while strategizing and plotting, you watch a plague of rats stagger around the office. They are also foaming at the mouth, so you presume they were poisoned, but it's actually quite nice to know that animals have an afterlife too…

Eventually, you slap your hands down on your thighs, stand up and announce: 'Right!' The vermin flinch and promptly disappear, but you barely notice — you've got a decision to make.

You could hang around the offices and try and use your ghostly ways to make the suspects reveal something (turn to **242**) or you could head to the conference room in which the interviews for your replacement are happening (turn to **107**).

Alternatively, seeing as Jan has just picked his laptop up and is setting out — destination unknown! — you could follow him (turn to **67**).

214

Which is where the post has been deposited onto a small cupboard next to the door. However, there's been a mishap and the top letter is actually addressed to the company that works downstairs. Now, that's a thought! You didn't often have a reason to venture downstairs, but your current social life (pardon the pun!) is not exactly brimming with opportunities, so it might be interesting to broaden your horizons. No doubt, it's Robert's job to sort out the mail, but what if you could 'persuade' either Theo or Adam to take the letter downstairs — that might be a way to get a new angle on things!

You can only persuade Theo and Adam if you have ticked the codeword MIASMA, and if you can't or don't want to use this power, then nature will take its usual course, meaning Robert will deliver the letter.

So, who takes the mail downstairs?

Theo	Turn to **271**
Adam	Turn to **36**
Robert	Turn to **145**

215

It's an impersonal workplace though. Just two monitors, a docking station, keyboard and mouse adorn the surface. No photos, no fidget toys, no unwashed cups, nothing. But then you see the cactus perched on the adjacent set of drawers...

'Trevor! Trevor the prickly pear!'

This was, indeed, your desk, and if you haven't done so yet, tick the codeword **TREVOR**.

You slump into the chair that is adjusted specifically for your height, even though you can't actually feel the cushion underneath. Maybe there were other personal items, but they've been cleared away. Did your loved ones collect them as mementos? Do you have any loved ones?

But you still do not have the answers to these questions. You don't even know what your job was? You try to open the drawers, but your hand passes straight through, which doesn't make sense, seeing as you haven't passed through the chair, but what do you know about being dead?

There's nothing more to be achieved here, but if you have already met Monica, turn to **284**.

If you haven't, then you decide to check out the other (now-occupied) desk (turn to **237)**.

216

You drift along the back corridor towards the vaulted office but suddenly lose the ability to drift in a straight line and, like an astronaut on the space station, you start to bounce against and ricochet off the wall. Naturally, you reach out a hand to steady yourself…

If you have ticked the codeword CAUL, turn to **124** but **remember** that you were on your way to see the **weaselly man**!

If you haven't ticked CAUL, you manage to control your movement and reach your desired destination. Turn to **33**.

217

But before you reach her office, you see Marta heading towards the storeroom and the door slams shut before you can get in. If you have ticked:

ECTOPLASM   Turn to **90**
ECTOPLASM *and* CAUL Turn to **149**

If not, there's nothing you can do but wait outside the storeroom. You can faintly hear her talking — she must be on her phone — and after ten minutes, she exits and goes back to her desk! Oh well. You can now check out Hannah (turn to **37**), but if you've already done that, then turn to **13**.

218

It's a reasonable suggestion. If anyone was going to find out Marta's secret thieving, it would be the Office Manager. Saving one's own skin is a common enough motive for murder, but that's not the case here. Marta was pretty confident that Robert didn't have a clue what was happening under his nose **Add 5 PURGATORY** points, then turn to **150**.

219

Although you're deep in thought, you got enough wits left to notice the packet of cigarettes on the shelf opposite. That's unusual, so you give it a poke and to your amazement, your finger doesn't go straight through — the packet moves! That's got to be useful, so you grab the **spectral cigarettes**, wait for the ectoplasm to build up again, then leave.

Marta is back at her desk, so you can now check out Adam (turn to **278**) or Hannah (turn to **72**). But if you've already done that, then drift towards the landing to think about your strategy (turn to **63**).

220

You wander into the lounge area, but it's just as boring here — no one is chatting, so you can't pick up any interesting gossip! However, before you get too disheartened, if you have ticked the codeword ECTOPLASM, you should turn to **184**. If you haven't, then turn to **74**.

221

Unsurprisingly, the assistant is glued to a tablet, swiping, scrolling and typing with manic efficiency. Why he is doing this is not exactly clear, until he bumps into Theo.

'Oh, hi. I've not taken your order yet; I'm getting everyone's lunch from the Asian place in the concourse. I emailed you the menu — have you had chance to check it out? I hear the Tom Kha Gai is pretty good.'

Theo smiles, then arches an eyebrow.

'Only if you want to kill me! I'm allergic to coconut milk. No, I'll have the tofu Kaeng Pa. Your boss is Kelsey, is she free? I'll love to have a chat about opportunities.' Tick **CLUE 7**.

Abruptly, the assistant's mask of professionalism slips, revealing a slightly panic-stricken grimace.

'No, no, she's not free at the moment. She just needs some time out for... something... anyhow, I better go get the order!'

And with an air of desperation, he heads for the stairs. If you want to **escape** with him, then you should know what to do **now**.

If not, then you must go to the Conference Room — the 'fireside chat' is about to start! Turn to **104**.

222

This is a sensible suggestion — Louisa was definitely worried that you knew something about her past. Did she silence you to prevent a dramatic revelation? Actually, she didn't. However, she did give you an undeserved promotion to keep you sweet (and at the same time, getting one over on Hannah in retaliation for the nasty comments!).

Add 5 PURGATORY points, then turn to **150**.

223

You peer over his shoulder, watching as he goes light-headed for a split second, and read the first statement.

Favourite film is "John Wick"

You and Theo both purse your lips as you weigh up the possibilities. Who do you think Theo should talk to first? Who do you think is the violent revenge film afficionado?

Hannah	Turn to **53**
Robert	Turn to **110**
Jan	Turn to **239**
Marta	Turn to **194**
Adam	Turn to **69**

224

With a rippling ghostly fart, you make Jan press the desk height adjuster button. Theo watches as the desk rises until it finally smacks into Jan's chin and the trance is broken.

'What are you doing?'

But Jan doesn't answer, he just looks confused. Meanwhile, you are under the desk, trying to spot whatever fell from the underneath of the desk as it rose.

Ah-ha, there it is! It's a key! If you earlier found a phantasmagorically locked door, then you would also know the 4-digit number that was etched onto it.

Reverse the number, then take the **middle two digits** and head to the section with the same number — for example, if the 4-digit number was 4827, you would turn to 28 [4827 becomes 7**28**4] — but **remember this section**, as you will return here afterwards.

Regardless of whether you've just returned from the locked door or you never found it in the first place, you can now either check out Hannah (turn to **37**) or Marta (turn to **217**), but if you've already done that, then turn to **13**.

225

Seven people enter the conference room and take their seats, leaving one empty chair. Yours, you presume. And suddenly, seeing all of them together, you have a blast of recall.

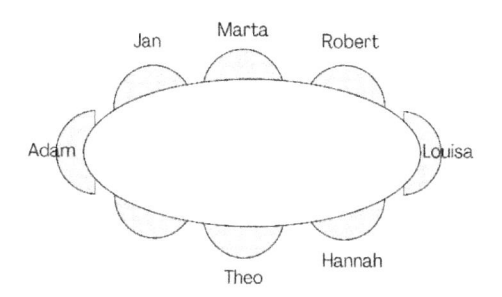

```
              Marta
       Jan            Robert
    ⌒   ⌒   ⌒
  ⌒               ⌒
 Adam              Louisa
  ⌒               ⌒
    ⌒   ⌒   ⌒
             Hannah
       Theo
```

Well, now you know their names, and although it's obvious that Louisa is the boss, you are still clueless as to what their jobs are or what this company even does.

    'So, I just wanted to let you know — short notice, I'm afraid, head office has only just informed me — but the funeral is this afternoon and whoever wants to go, is given 4 hours PTO to do so.'

As she talks, you glide around the table, peeking at the open laptops.

Hannah and Jan are sending emails; Theo looks half asleep; Marta is checking the Teams chat and Adam is Googling how to solve some programming bug. The lack of compassion is a bit galling; you just hope that you have family and friends who are more upset by your demise than this lot! Only Robert is paying attention, but if you're being honest, it looks like he just wants to impress Louisa. Fed up with gliding, you decide to settle somewhere for the rest of this meeting, but do you want to hover near the unit with the fancy objet d'arts and large screen (turn to **22**) or sit in your 'old' seat (turn to **142**)?

226

Even though your computer has already been cleaned and rebooted for the next unfortunate schmuck who works here, the memory is so vivid, it's like you're back at your desk. You can even feel the sticky TAB key…

But despite opening the browser and expecting some miraculous revelation to happen, nothing really does.

But the next thing you know is you've gone down so many rabbit holes — unusual deaths (well, you do have a vested interest), videos of rug cleaning (very satisfying) and lists of lists! — that it is now the middle of the night and the office is empty.

The hallucination of your laptop has gone too, so you are left with contemplating your next move. But that depends on whether you've ticked the codeword TELEPORTATION or not. If you have ticked it, turn to **259** and if not, turn to **13**.

227

It was the logical choice — there is literally an ESC key on it! Make a note that when you are given an opportunity to **ESCAPE** from the office, you must **add 65** to the section you are at.

However, the ESC key needs to be pressed and that's a bit more difficult. Three times you watch your entire hand sink through the keyboard and desk before wondering whether there's a way to make Jan press it. Aiming for a telepathic connection, you concentrate very hard. With your non-existent breath being held and furrowed brow, you simply look as though you're straining to go to the toilet, so it should come as no surprise when a spectral fart comes out. It's a tiny, odourless 'parp', but Jan suddenly looks around, mutters, 'What the…?' and inexplicably presses the ESC key. The ability to make the Living do what you want is a useful, albeit short-lived, skill to have, so ignore the embarrassment and tick the codeword **MIASMA**.

'Blimey! Was that you.?'

The voice echoes in your ear — it's that close! — and you shriek and run away, right through Marta!

'Bloody Hell!' both she and the new ghost shout, but whereas Marta looks unsettled, new ghost with his eighties' hairstyle, wild-staring eyes and white powdered nose, just laughs hysterically. Record that you have met **CHARLIE**.

'You know, if you like, we can photocopy your bum too.'

The last thing you want to do is office pranks with this hyperactive spectre, besides, you now feel an unpleasant pull on your intestines — or, at least, where your intestines used to be. Is this just the aftermath of your gas or did it work?

Jan then stands up and says, 'See you later,' to Marta, who doesn't seem keen to start work and is now casually leaning against the huge photocopier which stands in the corner of their office. She says, 'Be sensible!' as he exits the office. And like a balloon tethered to a child, you bob along after him.

It worked! Turn to **185**.

228

There's no mysterious vanishing for you this night. You stay wide awake, fuming and cursing with each hour that passes until finally, the sun rises, and you hear the sound of high heels coming up the stairs.

Hannah has barely got her coat off, when all your pent-up rage explodes. You are so angry that the energy manifests not only a semi-transparent image of you, but also a poltergeist-like chaos. Objects fly around the office before smashing against walls and furniture. A phone, a cup, a monitor! Even Trevor the prickly pear does not escape your fury as the plant pot is flung, terracotta shards and soil ricocheting over the floor.

Hannah is frozen in terror — white faced and staring — until she eventually recognises that you are shouting, 'You poisoned me! You poisoned me!'

She holds her hands up in a conciliatory gesture.

'No, no. I did give you the Thai curry, but I didn't buy it or make it myself. It was in burgundy

Tupperware, so I thought it was Louisa's. I thought she'd be really angry at you for taking her food. I wanted to get back at you. I didn't know it had paracetamol in it. You have to believe me!'

But that is the question: Do you believe her? Before you make your mind up about that, though, turn immediately to **73** if you discovered the TRUTH about Hannah.

If not, then you have a decision to make right now.

Do you think that Hannah ***did not*** put paracetamol in the curry (turn to **197**) or do you believe that she's lying in order to shift the blame off her own shoulders (turn to **299**)?

229

Jan? Of course, it wasn't Jan. He wasn't even in the office that day. He was having a secret job interview, so couldn't have brought in the paracetamol-laden food. Let's put that failed attempt down to a moment of spectral madness and try again.

Who brought the Thai curry into the office?

Robert	Turn to **2**
Louisa	Turn to **235**
Marta	Turn to **165**
Adam	Turn to **61**
Theo	Turn to **272**

230

The landing winds around to the right. It's a narrow corridor with tasteful art on one side and so-called privacy pods on the other. They are narrow, uncomfortable spaces with a tiny table, wall-mounted monitor and docking station for power and WLAN. They are also supposed to be soundproofed but— 'They weren't and we always used to moan about it!' You jump up and punch the air. You've remembered something! Nothing particularly exciting, you admit, but it's a start. However, while you're congratulating yourself, two things catch your eye. A freebie newspaper that's been left behind in the last pod and a ghost standing at the end of the corridor. What will you do first? Talk to the ghost (turn to **138**) or try to read the newspaper (turn to **76**)?

231

'Aah, perfect!' He grabs it out of your green hands and proceeds to search under the desk. When he finally emerges, he is successfully grasping a tiny white tablet.

'Thank goodness. It's the last of my morphine! Now then, you said you died recently. Has anyone told you about limbo?'

When you shake your head, he continues. 'Yes, it's a bit like clearing your ears after a flight. Just hold your nose, then blow until your ears pop, and then you'll have a flashback. It's only brief and some people are better than others at guiding the process, but it might be useful. However, most people can't recall their actual death or key points around it — too traumatic, so the brain blocks it. Now, I've chatted far too long. Go!' Tick the codeword **LIMBO**.

However, when you start to head back to the workers' room, he stands up again, bellowing in his wheezy fashion.

'Not that way! You'll disturb the workers. I don't know what they do, but they're busy and that's the main thing. Being busy!'

He opens up another door, shoves you through it, then slams it shut. As in a dream, you find yourself back in the narrow corridor. The door has now vanished, replaced by the exposed brick wall. That was an interesting digression but did it get you any closer to finding out who had the opportunity to give you the Thai curry? No, it did not! But all is not lost — how about trying out your new skill?

Turn to **167**.

232

She tries to keep quiet, but Louisa has a nagging thought that she can't leave alone. A thought concerning someone she used to work with…

'Did Ashley ever talk about me? About a previous job?'

It's an odd set of questions, which immediately sounds suspicious, but after a moment of confusion, your mum stares Louisa directly in the eyes.

'Ashley didn't like the way you treated Jan. I mean, she didn't like Jan by the end, but she always said there was no need for you to behave the way you did with him just because he's Polish.'

There is another long, drawn-out silence until Louisa asks, 'Did Ashley mention Astrid Pomeroy?'

'What?' And your mum looks completely bamboozled by the question. It's enough for Louisa to sigh with relief and usher your mum out. When she returns to her office, she sinks into her chair, muttering, 'Thank goodness, I didn't do anything more drastic than giving an underqualified person a job. She didn't even know I worked with Astrid!'

Despite bristling that she's called you 'underqualified' — how dare she! — you desperately want to hear a lengthier confession from Louisa, but she then strides out of the office and heads to the Conference Room — the 'fireside chat' is about to start! Turn to **104**.

233

With three people gone, the office is a bit boring. You rattle around, trying to manifest any spectral phenomena, but after a particularly embarrassing attempt to rattle a cup in the kitchen — you fall into the sink! — you decide to see what the remaining workers are up to. Whose office do you want to visit?

Theo and Robert	Turn to **295**
Hannah	Turn to **151**
Marta	Turn to **9**

234

With a flash, you remember what Mangled Ghost told you and it all fits into place. Not Martha, Aaron and Lightning Bolt cables, but Marta, Adam and Thunderbolt cables! He is the other one who knows her secret and whilst she isn't worried about Jan grassing her up, she must be concerned about Adam. After all, he would sell his grandmother if he thought it would benefit him!

You have discovered the **TRUTH about Marta**. Now return to your previous section, which was either **25** or **190**.

235

When you think about it, Louisa does make a good suspect. Paranoid about her past racist behaviour being revealed, while fending off accusations of current discriminations is bad enough but throw an illicit work affair into the mix, and you have all the ingredients for a desperate murderer. Plus, she has burgundy Tupperware! That's all well and good, but who do you think her intended victim was?

You	Turn to **222**
Hannah	Turn to **89**
Jan	Turn to **62**
Adam	Turn to **12**
Marta	Turn to **298**
Theo	Turn to **156**
Robert	Turn to **137**

236

Although it seemed like a good idea at the time, listening to people regurgitate the same old reasons that they should be hired quickly becomes boring. However, when the third interviewee is asked about examples in which they handled team conflicts, they mention a firm they once worked for and Louisa's reaction is telling…

You are sitting cross-legged on the table directly in front of her, so instantly witness her tension and hear the sudden intake of breath. There's a pause and then Louisa says somewhat frostily, 'Oh, I didn't see that on your CV. Did you work with Astrid Pomeroy?'

The poor interviewee smiles nervously, well aware that something has gone wrong but totally clueless as to what.

'No, I don't believe so, I think she left the company shortly before I joined.'

And with that, the tension lifts and they move onto the 'Have you any questions for us?' section.

Once it has finished, Louisa types up notes while Robert scrolls through Instagram on his phone — why is he even here? — and you realise that this could be a good opportunity to delve deeper into his backstory. However, you can only interact with his phone if you have ticked the codeword MIASMA.

If you have, turn to **82**.

If not, you've had enough of watching reels and, when the next interviewee comes in, you sneak through the gap to see what Theo is doing now (turn to **192**).

237

The woman is busy, clicking on various folders and tabs while dialling a number. But as you step towards the desk, there is a sudden, acrid smell of burnt plasticky fish in the air! A horrible swirl of atoms leaves you feeling like you've been in a washing machine, although you recover quickly enough to see the woman wrinkle her nose and mutter, 'Is something burning?'

Clearly, she's a consummate professional, so she ignores the prospect of being electrocuted or going up in flames and speaks to the person who has just answered her call.

'Good morning, Noah. Hannah here. Marketing Lead. Do you have a few minutes now? I'd love to run some proposals by you.'

And then everything starts to swirl again — maybe you need to really concentrate when you're dead. It's not like a Teams meeting where you can switch off your camera and play sudoku while it drones on. You try to focus on the woman again but can't help thinking that she said *Marketing Lead*. Now why was that gnawing at your mind? However, the swirling is verging on tornado strength, so you decide that a change of scenery is needed and leave the office (turn to **64**).

238

When a single drop plops off your finger, the exit door squeaks open and you peer out. At first, the service tunnel is empty, and the only thing you can see is the doorway opposite. There are no signs, but you know it opens up into the basement of the Thai café that you've visited now and then in the station concourse. And as you stare, you hear a distant thudding…

Which gets louder and louder until—

A horde of mutants burst into view, running along the service tunnel and into the actual Underground. A mass of weird, human-like creatures, but they are unrecognisable with massively enlarged heads and thin, wasted bodies. You gasp and draw back, but not before one spins around to face you, alerted by the sound. It launches forward, but the door is already closing under its own weight, and although there is a bone-shaking slam as it hits the door, it cannot reach you.

Tick the codeword **PREMONITION**.

'What was that?' you whisper in the dark. No one answers, though, so you shakily head back to the stairs — you've had enough of the basement for this afterlife! — but do you want to go via the normal stairs (turn to **260**) or the creepy, not-often-used back staircase (turn to **77**)?

239

With a tired sigh, Jan says, 'No.'

And that's all you're getting from him. No explanation, no embellishment, nothing!

Although you're quite happy to continue with the bingo, too many people are moving around this small space, making both time and the surroundings shift and judder. By the time everything settles again, Louisa is announcing the next activity. Turn to **275**.

240

A formal-looking document materialises out of thin air, then floats gently down to your feet. You pick it up and read. It's a written warning. Apparently, following a performance review, you have been evaluated as underperforming. There will be no further incremental pay increases — Pay? What pay? — and no opportunities for promotion until you demonstrate that you can be a reliable team member. You look around, confused and wondering how a haunting apparition can prove they're a team player, but then realise that time has passed. Marylebone Station is no more and there are just a few Rumba-like robots scooting across a vast concreted plain. Where has London gone?

Presumably, all your old office colleagues died long ago, including your murderer, so there's no chance of any justice for you. Look on the positive side, though — you still have a job!

Your game ends here!

241

NSFW Ghost claps his hands in undisguised amusement — Louisa and Robert are in the middle of a heated, yet muted, row!

'I can't believe you didn't tell me! Why didn't you tell me? She said what?'

'She told Ashley the curry was from you. You have that type of Tupperware. Was it you? Did you bring the curry in?'

'No! No, of course, I didn't. Since when do I bring in food for people?'

It's a good question and Robert is temporarily stumped, but Louisa carries on regardless.

'It was bad enough that she said those nasty things about me in the email, but I gave Ashley the job, so we were evens after that. There was no need to try and frame me for murder!'

Robert still hasn't got a reply, but luckily, someone knocks on Louisa's door. It's one of Head Office's nameless assistants.

'There's someone here for you. She says that she's Ashley's mom.'

Robert and Louisa grimace at each other, then Louisa nods.

'Show her in.'

To your amazement, your mum is here.

'I've come to pick up Ashley's stuff. Sorry it's taken me so long.'

Louisa looks uncomfortable but says that there isn't much to collect, as there was an incident and your prickly pear, amongst other things, was damaged. Your mum shrugs her shoulders, as though the worst has already happened, so a plant is of no real concern. An awkward silence then settles over the two women — who will break first?

If you have discovered the TRUTH about Louisa, turn to **232**, but if you haven't been privy to this information, turn to **202**.

242

But there aren't that many people actually working normally here today? So, who do you want to interrogate in your ghostly fashion first?

Adam	Turn to **278**
Hannah	Turn to **72**
Marta	Turn to **211**

243

NSFW Ghost is leering over Louisa's shoulder, trying to peek down her blouse, when you arrive in her office. He jumps and backs away, looking like a naughty schoolboy, but you've got bigger fish to fry. Louisa is sitting at her desk, eating chicken and steamed broccoli from a burgundy Tupperware bowl. It does not look appetising and NSFW Ghost agrees.

'It's like that every day. Only ever eats boring food because she's on a never-ending diet. But do you want to know a secret?'

You nod, lean closer, then realise his hand is slyly creeping to your rear. You smack it away and take a step back. It's not like you need to whisper any way!

'You can't blame a chap for trying. Anyhow, she's got a packet of biscuits hidden in her desk. When she thinks no one is around, she wolfs them. Four or five in one go.'

If you'd still been alive, you would have been totally entertained by this gossip, but instead, you snap, 'Is there anything else? Any feuds?'

'Well, she's got no time for the foreign bloke. Always bitching about him with the one she's having it away with. Well, was having it away with.' Tick both **CLUES 6 and 8**.

By now, Louisa has finished the last broccoli spear, then checks that no one is in the lounge area and grabs a couple of chocolate digestives. Just as NSFW Ghost said! Talking of which, he's disappeared, so what should you do next?

You could talk to:

Party Ghost	Turn to **208**
Beehive Ghost	Turn to **175**
Charlie	Turn to **108**

…but only if you've **previously met** them!

And if you've finished with the spectres, then you could check out the kitchen for any clues (turn to **35**), but if you've already done that, then tick the codeword **MEANS** and think about the next stage of your investigation.

If you've ticked the codeword OPPORTUNITY, turn to **246**, if not, turn to **6**.

244

You are definitely running out of options — how are you going to get Robert to reveal what and who he heard on your last day in the office? Maybe you need to scare him into a confession…

If you have acquired a pair of phantom shoes, turn to **30**, but if not, turn to **49**.

245

You had concentrated so much on trying to get Hannah to go towards Jan, you accidentally let out a tiny fart. If you haven't done so yet, you can now tick the codeword **MIASMA**.

'A second language? I'm Polish, so of course I speak a second language. This is ridiculous!'
He's clearly irritated by the team bonding, but Hannah doesn't join in. She's keeping it strictly professional!
You then realise that Hannah has written the number "**7**" on her card, which is weird, and although you're quite happy to continue with the bingo, too many people are moving around this small space, making both time and the surroundings shift and judder. By the time everything settles again, Louisa is announcing the next activity. Turn to **275**.

246

But before you can plot the next steps, you see Adam march officiously into the lounge area, laptop held open on one forearm and a cup of coffee in his free hand. He's heading towards Louisa's office for his biweekly one-to-one session. That might be worth joining, but Hannah and Theo are having a water cooler moment in the corner of the room. They look cagey, so eavesdropping on that conversation could be interesting. You can't be in two places at the same time, so who do you choose to spy on?

> Adam's one-to-one   Turn to **87**
> Hannah and Theo's chat   Turn to **139**

247

The photo doesn't ring any bells though. You can't remember where you met her. Did you become friends because you worked with Robert? Did you introduce her to Robert? Oh, so many questions…

Despite your spooky powers, Robert puts his phone down as the next interviewee comes in, so you decide to sneak through the gap to see what Theo is doing now (turn to **192**).

248

The woman — mid-forties with an air of bossiness — reaches the landing first and makes a big fuss of taking her coat off, which is a sly tactic to disguise that she's out of breath. She then marches away down the corridor. Close behind is a younger man. With sandy-blond hair and skin too pale to tan, there is something familiar about him. He gives a condescending sneer behind the woman's back, then heads past the kitchen and into another office.

Do you want to follow him (turn to **28**) or find the woman (turn to **129**)?

249

As you approach, they all turn to face you, smiling expectantly. But on a closer inspection, it's clear that these smiles are fixed grimaces. They look gaunt and grey-skinned — are they ever given a break so they can eat or sleep? — yet still desperately trying to impress. Poor things! One of them pushes through to the front and presents an object to you, saying, 'I found this and thought it might come in handy, which is a good example of how I can think on my feet and always put the company first.' The others nearby hear this and actually growl at him. Blimey! Competition is certainly fierce here!

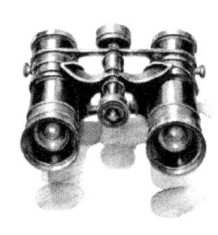

You take the object and back away, keen to put some distance between you and them, in case a fight breaks out. Make a note that you are now the proud owner of **vintage opera glasses**. It's quite a relief when you see someone beckoning you over. He looks like he's the boss, so you'd better obey! Turn to **117**.

250

Channelling all the true crime programmes you ever watched, you hone in on MMO as the key to solving your murder — motive, means and opportunity! But before you make any concrete plans, an even more obvious solution occurs to you. Why not ask the other ghosts? Surely one of them was haunting your office and saw who gave you the Thai curry. It's a good idea but will only work if you actually know where you worked. Have you ticked the codeword TREVOR?

If you have, turn to **97**, but if not, turn to **144**.

251

It's a sensible suggestion; the two men did share an office, so Robert might have discovered Theo's dark and illegal secret. But let's be honest — Robert is not the sharpest knife in the drawer and Theo knew that he was no threat.

Add 5 PURGATORY points, then turn to **150**.

252

At first, you are confused. Normally, when you look out of a window, you see the outside — surely the afterlife isn't so different! — but this is a station concourse…

With a flash, the memory pops into your head. It's London. Marylebone Station to be precise. You lived in London, and the offices where you worked were in the station building itself. How on Earth could I afford that, you wonder, as you watch the people below. A never-ending stream of bodies heading to or from the platforms, but then you realise that some have stopped and are staring up at you. A cyclist with a dented, blood-stained helmet, a woman wearing a long, old-fashioned skirt which is torn, revealing her amputated leg, a young man with a blade protruding from the front of his tracksuit top. And between them all, a fluttering, untethered, **American-style police tape**. Why on Earth is that there?

POLICE LINE DO NOT CROSS POLICE LINE DO NOT CROSS

As you watch, more and more stop. The dead of the station, you presume and feel decidedly depressed.

'Why haven't they moved on?' you snap, before remembering that no one can hear you anymore. You step away from the window and, for a second, hope to catch your own reflection, but no. You're invisible as well as silent.

It's probably best not to dwell on that, but luckily there is a handy distraction. The door opens again and, with a clatter of high, yet professional, heels, a young woman enters the office, then plonks her bag on the other desk. She swiftly brings out a laptop, then sits down. No prevaricating for her — she's straight down to business! If only you knew who she was…

Next, you could check out the desk that the man was looking in (turn to **171**) or the other (now-occupied) desk (turn to **237**).

253

There really wasn't any evidence to suggest that Robert wanted Adam dead, as irritating as he is… **Add 15 PURGATORY** points, then turn to **150**.

254

Really? You weren't aware of the professional rivalry between Adam and Theo? That's surprising, as the mutual hatred simmered during every interaction! **Add 5 PURGATORY** points.

Both men thought they were the alpha at work, only Theo was the actual Team Lead, and that was a source of intense jealousy for Adam. Remember, how he kept trying to promote himself. Yes, he wanted Theo gone so he could take his rightful place. But what was Adam's plan?

If you have ticked CLUE 10, turn to **102**. If not, turn to **50**.

255

Another drop of ectoplasm, and you are inside the server room. A sudden memory hits you — you were in here once before when the internet inexplicably died and a group of you squeezed in to stare at the router. Nobody knew what they were doing, of course, and the internet returned on its own accord after half an hour — however, you're absolutely certain that it didn't smell like this! An intense stench of hot, greasy, charred flesh fills your nostrils, making you gag. And as if that isn't bad enough, you hear a voice saying, 'Who's left this open?' then the door is slammed shut.

Mid-retches, you try to summon up more ectoplasm, but it's no good. Maybe there's a limit on how much you can conjure up in such a short space of time…

You sink to your knees, both hands clamped firmly over your mouth and nostrils, but thankfully, the door opens again, and Theo strides in. Both you and the fresh air are swirled around, but as you settle, you hear him mutter, 'This better not be Adam bloody messing with things again.' There is no love lost between those two, it seems. Tick **CLUE 5**.

After a cursory check, Theo exits the server room, and you gratefully leave too. Turn to **277**.

256

Charlie hangs around Marta and Jan's office and if they're celebrating, it must mean one thing — Jan got the job! Despite the breakup, you are genuinely pleased for him and know that Jan had no reason to murder you and wasn't even in the office that day. Do you want to spend this opportunity confirming what you already know? If you want to hear Marta and Jan's celebration, turn to **11**, but if not, you can choose a different ghost to check-in with.

However, you must have **previously met** them!

NSFW Ghost	Turn to **241**
Pale Ghost	Turn to **122**

But if they're not an option, then you should investigate what the COO's minion is up to.
Turn to **221**.

257

The next thing you know, you're standing at a window, staring out at the station concourse. Amongst the commuters and tourists, you spot a dead horse. 'What did it do wrong to have to spend decades here?' you wonder, then collect yourself. You still have a poisoning to solve! But before you can gather your thoughts, the noise from the rest of the office piques your curiosity.

Today is clearly not a normal office day — it's a Head Office Visit day! Louisa is running around like a headless chicken and everyone else is either following her instructions or hiding. This should be interesting…

Meredith (CEO), Justin (CFO) and Kelsey (COO), plus their minions, are here, and they want to have not only individual meet-and-greets but also a 'fireside chat'! Blimey!

You're not sure if anything useful will come to light during the day, but you ask the other ghosts if they can listen out and let you know if there's something juicy going on. However, only the ghosts that you've **already met** will agree to this, and if you've met all of them, then you'll have to make a choice — despite being a phantom, you can't be in two places at once! **Remember, though: if a ghost has moved on from this spectral plane, then they are simply not here to do this favour for you.**

> NSFW Ghost   Turn to **268**
> Charlie   Turn to **58**
> Pale Ghost   Turn to **296**

However, if you haven't really made any phantom friends yet, then you should hang around the Conference Room. Something interesting is bound to happen, sooner or later, isn't it? Turn to **169**.

258

When you grab the WLAN cable, the screen bursts into life and your message — ENOUGH! OR ELSE! — is emblazoned for all to see.

Theo's face goes as pale as putty, but he quickly recovers to fiddle with the on/off button, eventually sighing with relief as the screen goes black again.

The interviewees have fixed grins on their faces, so Theo decides to act as if nothing unusual has just happened, answering his own rhetorical question about sour grapes.

    'Possibly, but who knows?'

    'Is there a lot of rivalry here or does the team get on?' One of them finally asks.

'Healthy competition, I would say. Some people need to know their place though — not everyone has the right credentials to be departmental Leads!'

At this point, the conference door opens and everyone hushes. Which is why you hear the tiny tinkle of something metallic falling from the back of the screen, presumably loosened by Theo's fumbling.

It's a key! If you earlier found a phantasmagorically locked door, then you would also know the 4-digit number that was etched onto it.

Reverse the number, then take the **middle two digits** and head to the section with the same number — for example, if the 4-digit number was 4827, you would turn to 28 [4827 becomes 7**28**4] — but **remember this section**, as you will return here afterwards.

Regardless of whether you've just returned from the locked door or you never found it in the first place, you now decide to see how the interviews are going. Turn to **236**.

259

The following day you wait impatiently for everyone to arrive so you carry on with your investigations, but it appears that you've timed this badly. Robert has PTO, Louisa has a meeting somewhere in London, and Adam has called in sick! It's not a total lost cause though — you can check out Marta (turn to **217**), Hannah (turn to **37**) or if you haven't had enough of Jan, you can see what he's doing today — for some reason, he's in the vaulted office with Theo! Turn to **157**.

260

Along the way, you float past a cleaner's trolley and notice something odd wedged between a bottle of glass cleaner and a replacement mop head — it's a crumpled box of chocolates! You can just about make out a gift card attached and read:

> "My darling L, We deserve another chance. Don't give up on us! R"

Tick **CLUE 8**.

However, it looks like "L" threw the chocolates in the bin, so that doesn't bode well for true love! Still, at least the cleaner is benefiting from it. You carry on until reaching the entrance foyer. Have you already met the ghost called Clara?

If you have, turn to **94**, but if not, turn to **181**.

261

Presumably, it was a nice service but seeing as you fell asleep (or whatever it is that ghosts do), you missed it and only come around when Jan is leaving. Just in time to hear your father snap, 'Why have you come?'

You sense Jan bristle at this, but he manages to force a sombre nod, then replies, 'I have nothing to hide and I wanted to pay my respects.' His Polish accent becomes more pronounced, which you assume is due to nerves. 'It was a tragic accident to someone I thought a lot of, even though we weren't a couple anymore.'

It sounds heartfelt and honest, but if looks could kill…

Jan quickly and sensibly moves on before this turns into a stand-off, and however much you'd like to stay to find out why your parents had such a vehement reaction to him, you are linked to Jan and when he goes to the car park, you go too. It's an awkward meeting between him, Louisa and Adam — they can hardly ignore each other! — but while Jan is explaining that he's taking the train to meet with a client before heading back to the office, you spot a strange woman who is staring in your direction. You look around to see what's caught her eye and notice a group of battered, tattered musicians. Maybe you've got enough time to go and investigate one of these oddities, but who?

The strange woman (turn to **160**) or the musicians (turn to **273**)?

262

You hand over the vinyl record and when Beehive Ghost sees the cover — Cilla Black on a garish yellow background, which reminds you of your jaundiced skin! — she gasps in delight.

'Oh, I loved this. I absolutely loved it. Thank you so much. Oh, I must do something in return,' and she clasps the record to her chest while she concentrates. Eventually, she looks up.

'I know! There was this one occasion when you came into this office and said that a bloke from downstairs had asked you if you knew anything about DataFusion, and that there was something going on with his co-workers and Theo. Now, at that point, Theo went pale. I thought he was about to pass out, but when you said that you'd told him that you don't know what he was talking about, Theo looked so relieved. He tried to act all casual and said it was just an idea, just talk between nerds and you frowned, said that you couldn't care less but could he stop his friends from harassing you!'

If you have already discovered the TRUTH about Theo, turn to **96**. If not, turn to **173**.

263

Adam did accidentally learn of Marta's thieving that day in the basement, but that is no reason for him to kill her. Which is why he didn't.

Add 10 PURGATORY points, then turn to **195**.

264

'Are you alright?'

You open your eyes to the strange sight of a sideways head peering at you and realise that you're lying at the bottom of the stairs.

'You stayed out too long, didn't you?' Clara's voice is slightly chiding, but she gives you an understanding pat on your shoulder, which has, thankfully, reappeared.

'You're not the first ghost and you won't be the last, but we all rebound back here as soon as we've vanished completely.'

You can see the station clock through the door and realise that it's evening — you've wasted a whole day of investigating! Still, it's not all bad. You know now that Jan has been skipping work to go for interviews behind Louisa's back. There was a slim chance that Jan was worried that you knew and was going to grass him up, but he wasn't in the office on that day, so couldn't have given you the Thai curry. You have discovered the **TRUTH about Jan**.

However, you recognised the other voice on the phone — Marta has been in on this secret and even helped him out with a fake reference. So, was she doing his dirty work for him and making sure that you didn't spoil his job search?

You say this to Clara and she looks distinctly unimpressed.

'I'm not sure how much things have changed since my death but would someone really murder another person just over an interview?'

She has a point — it's not the usual crime of passion, that's for sure. Feeling that you'd like to get something else out of this day, you ask if anyone is still in the office and to your surprise, she nods.

'Yes, the boss woman and the weaselly man.' That's dedication! So, who would you like to visit?

Boss woman	Turn to **178**
Weaselly man	Turn to **33**

265

It's not a bad idea. Adam knew about her thieving, so Marta may have felt compelled to silence the only witness to her crimes. However, she also felt pretty confident that, if he ever spilt the beans about her, she could spin a good line and no one would believe Adam, the perennial liar. The risk of being outed as a thief was not high enough to justify murder!
Add 5 PURGATORY points, then turn to **150**.

266

The conclusion is clear — even if Robert was scared that you might tell his wife — your friend! — about his affair with Louisa, he didn't actually do anything about it.

Think about it — if he had brought the curry in, he wouldn't be conflicted over whether Louisa had laced it or not. He would ***know*** that she hadn't put paracetamol in it!

Feeling overwhelmed, you stop walking and take the shoes off. In the sudden silence, Robert wipes the tears from his cheeks, now embarrassed with his performance, but as he exits the office, he mutters, 'It was Hannah.'

You wait, wondering if this breakthrough is what's needed to catapult you into a better afterlife, but nothing happens. Instead, you hunker down to await Hannah's return tomorrow. Turn to **228**.

267

You're absolutely convinced that you know where the prize is and glide through the office until reaching the conference room. However, Robert and Adam must have gone somewhere else! Seconds later, you hear a triumphant shout and realise that they found the prize and you didn't!

There's no time to be peeved about it though, as Louisa is wrapping up the team bonding session. And not a moment too soon. She looks like she's going to spend her lunch break in the nearest wine bar! Everyone heads either to their desks or the toilet, and you end up floating aimlessly in the large, vaulted office. Turn to **214**.

268

NSFW Ghost claps his hands in undisguised amusement — Louisa and Robert are in the middle of a heated, yet muted, row!

'I can't believe you didn't tell me! Why didn't you tell me? She said what?'

'She told Ashley the curry was from you. You have that type of Tupperware. Was it you? Did you bring the curry in?'

'No! No, of course, I didn't. Since when do I bring in food for people?'

It's a good question and Robert is temporarily stumped, but Louisa carries on regardless.

'It was bad enough that she said those nasty things about me in the email, but I gave Ashley the job, so we were evens after that. There was no need to try and frame me for murder!'

Robert still hasn't got a reply, but luckily, someone knocks on Louisa's door. It's one of Head Office's nameless assistants.

'There's someone here for you. She says that she's Ashley's mom.'

Robert and Louisa grimace at each other, then Louisa nods.

'Show her in.'

To your amazement, your mum is here.

'I've come to pick up Ashley's stuff. Sorry it's taken me so long.'

Louisa looks uncomfortable but says that there isn't much to collect, as there was an incident and your prickly pear, amongst other things, was damaged. Your mum shrugs her shoulders, as though the worst has already happened, so a plant is of no real concern. An awkward silence then settles over the two women — who will break first?

If you have discovered the TRUTH about Louisa, turn to **116**, but if you haven't been privy to this information, turn to **174**.

269

You drift along the back corridor towards Louisa's office but suddenly lose the ability to drift in a straight line and, like an astronaut on the space station, you start to bounce against and ricochet off the wall. Naturally, you reach out a hand to steady yourself…

If you have ticked the codeword CAUL, turn to **124** but **remember** that you were on your way to see the **boss woman**!

If you haven't ticked CAUL, you manage to control your movement and make it to the desired destination. Turn to **178**.

270

Mangled Ghost nods enthusiastically (or maybe that's just his partial decapitation) and says, 'For sure! They come in, park or unlock their bikes, then go.'

'Is that all?'

'Well, there was this one time. A woman, Martha, maybe, she was getting her bike and dropped all these cables that she had stuffed in her jacket. I used to do that with bottles of vodka, so I think she'd stolen them. Anyway, a man appeared. Was he called Aaron? Something like that. He saw and helped her pick them up, but she didn't seem happy with that. He said they were… Lightning Bolts. No, but something like that. Does that help?'
Tick **CLUE 11**.

You try to commit all this to memory, but when you think of an important follow-up question, realise that he's vanished!

As you're down here, it would make sense to have a look around, but do you want to check out the rest of the bicycle section (turn to **26**) or the nearby boiler room (turn to **131**)?

271

Sounding like a balloon popping, the spectral fart echoes around the office, and Theo purposefully marches to the door and snatches up the mail. You glide after him, down the steep stairs, around the corner and into the offices below. The layout is similar but with a brand colour scheme of chocolate brown and teal, and promotional posters of happy, smiling people. It's really not clear what their business is — something to do with dentistry, perhaps? — but then again, you still don't remember what your own company does!

Theo drops the mail wordlessly on a nearby table, looks confused, then turns to leave, but just then, a man pops his head out of the adjacent office.

'Oh, it's you. It's been a while, how are you doing?'

'Oh hi, yes, I've not been avoiding you, I just thought it was better to keep my distance until the dust settled.'

The man looks shiftily around, then edges a little closer and murmurs, 'I think they've dropped the action. Seeing as the start-up was in Danesh's name, with his suicide and the complete cessation of business activity, they've lost interest. As far as I can tell…'

'Yes, well, it's not your neck on the block, is it? You weren't the one stealing IP!' That last part is hissed with particular venom, which is a side you've not seen so far — Theo is normally jokey and laid-back — then he hastily wraps up the conversation and heads back upstairs.

This must have been serious corporate counterfeiting! Tick **CLUE 12**. Quite how it fits with your murder, you have no idea, but any information could be useful. And just then, you notice something else. A slightly ajar door…

It's probably nothing, but while you're here, you might as well check it out. Turn to **206**.

272

OK, so underneath that breezy, cheeky persona, there were hints of stress and a desperate cover-up. Could Theo really have planted the poisoned curry? Has Theo ever owned a single piece of Tupperware? These are good questions, but the most important is: Who would he try to kill?

You	Turn to **164**
Hannah	Turn to **101**
Jan	Turn to **288**
Adam	Turn to **39**
Marta	Turn to **8**
Louisa	Turn to **204**
Robert	Turn to **251**

273

As you approach, the three young men adopt 'cool' poses, which is ridiculous considering that they have plainly been dead for four decades! Knowing you probably don't have long, you cut to the chase.

'How come you're still here?'

'We were driving back from a gig. We're Neon Blitz, you've probably heard of us.' The proverbial tumbleweed goes by while you stare perplexed until finally saying, 'No'.

Embarrassed but undaunted, Gus (lead guitarist, apparently) explains that their transit van crashed on this empty stretch of road because the driver (Vince, drummer) was drunk. However, he was wearing a seatbelt and survived, but the others were kipping in the back and were hit by flying amps in the carnage.

'We don't know how to move on. Well, we do, we need to go towards the light, but how do you do that in a field?'

It's a fair question, but just as you are about to respond, the tether snaps taut, and you are pulled off your feet and away. And in the blink of an eye, you are back in the office. Turn to **115**.

274

You hold your finger out and wait for the ectoplasm to start dripping, but nothing! The green algae that's still coated over your hands must be blocking it! Damn! There's nothing you can do but wait outside the storeroom.

You can faintly hear Marta talking — she must be on her phone — and after ten minutes, she exits and goes back to her desk! Oh well. You can now check out Adam (turn to **278**) or Hannah (turn to **72**). But if you've already done that, then drift towards the landing to think about your strategy (turn to **63**).

275

'And, of course, the winning pair will get a small prize!' Louisa announces. She's aiming for an impish delivery to show just how much fun this is, but it just comes across as slightly desperate and demented. There are some muted sighs and forced smiles as your ex-colleagues look over the clues and begin the Treasure Hunt.

You swirl around the office, not really following anyone in particular, but then realise that Adam and Robert are getting close to finding the prize. Curiosity piqued, you peer at their final clue…

> **BETWEEN THE INFRARED AND RADIO I LIE**

If you know where they should go, then turn to the office floor plan in **Appendix B** (The Office Floor Plan) at the back of the book so you can identify which grid the Treasure Hunt prize is hidden in?

- A5   Turn to **267**
- C1   Turn to **113**
- B2   Turn to **155**
- D3   Turn to **59**

276

Yes, Hannah did mock Adam about his ridiculous penchant for exaggerations and lies, but she was careful to do that behind his back. Adam had no reason to be aggrieved with her.

Add 10 PURGATORY points, then turn to **195**.

277

A polite cough tells you that you are not alone in the lounge area, but you are quite unprepared for this spectre! Blood trickles from both his eyes and nose and the back of his head is simply missing. The skull is a crater with brain matter erupting from its depths.

'I'd just been conscripted, but the Great War had been going for two years, and we all knew that fighting for King and country wasn't as heroic as we were led to believe. This—' and he gestures to the gaping wound, '—might not be pretty, but it was better than the alternative, I'm sure,' he says with a clipped, plummy accent.

'Right,' you agree politely, but then can't think of anything else to say. An awkward silence descends until Conscripted Ghost taps the nearest table with his shotgun.

'Let's sit. I'd like to help you. The others here can be redundant, if you ask me.'

You nod enthusiastically, happy to get any advice.

'There's got to be a reason why you're still here and random objects tend to point the way. Things that will mean something to you and your situation but not to others. Now then, think back.

Have you seen any incongruous items? Heard odd songs? Things that make you go, "Goodness me, why on Earth is that here?" Well, have you?'

You stare, dumbfounded, so he tuts and carries on.

'There will be something that links the objects. It could be their material, colour or perhaps a connection with a certain person or place.'

You rack your brain, replaying every step since you started haunting the office.

So, what one word links the objects seen here. Which connecting feature to they have in common? **Use the alphabet code at the start of the book (*Codewords*) to convert this word to a number, then turn to that section number.**

For example, if you think the connecting feature is that they are all BOOKS, you add up:

2 + 15 + 15 + 11 + 19 = 62

And then you would turn to section 62.

If you have no idea about any random objects and what they have in common, turn to **109**.

278

You find Adam at his desk. He's wound up and muttering to himself about Theo.

'Thinks he's the bee's knees. Chatting up the newbies, like he's the boss.'

You're not expecting anything else to be revealed, but when he unlocks his computer, he heads straight to his file explorer and opens up a PowerPoint. It looks like they're slides for a product update — didn't Theo, as Developer Lead, do all the presentations? And you could not imagine Theo giving Adam any kind of career-boost! So why does Adam have this PowerPoint?

You're not going to get the answer to that because he then shuts it down with a frustrated curse and continues working on his current programming project. Interesting! You're about to go and haunt someone else when a ghost materialises in the office. Have you already met Beehive Ghost?

| Yes | Turn to **66** |
| No | Turn to **152** |

279

Hmm, that would be ironic, wouldn't it? Robert bringing in poisoned curry for Hannah, only to hear her give it to someone else. But why would he want to kill Hannah, anyway? Well, there's absolutely no reason, so **add 15 PURGATORY** points, then turn to **150**.

280

Well, he didn't make a song and dance about it, but Theo had a serious allergy to coconut. In fact, a whiff of coconut would send him into an anaphylactic shock. There were many occasions when Theo refused to consume coconut — the pina colada, the Bounty bars, and the Tom Kha Gai — but maybe you missed that.

Add 5 PURGATORY points.

The Thai curry was made with coconut milk, and he probably thought about stealing it in the burgundy Tupperware, but one look would have made him abandon that idea instantly! Which is why it remained in the fridge until Hannah saw it and thought, 'This must be Louisa's lunch. How about getting Ashley to eat it as revenge for the promotion sabotage?' Turn to **70**.

281

You had concentrated so much on trying to get Robert to go towards Marta, you accidentally let out a tiny fart. If you haven't done so yet, you can now tick the codeword **MIASMA**.

'Yes, it's me, but seriously — who doesn't love a curry?' Marta then pauses, looking like she was going to say something derogatory about the team bonding but had second thoughts. So, with mutual nods, they look around for other people to talk to.

You then realise that Robert has written the number "**7**" on his card, which is weird, and although you're quite happy to continue with the bingo, too many people are moving around this small space, making both time and the surroundings shift and judder. By the time everything settles again, Louisa is announcing the next activity. Turn to **275**.

282

You peer over his shoulder, seeing him sniff a sudden, strange odour, and read the first statement.

Has probably eaten chocolate this morning

You and Jan both tut as you weigh up the possibilities. Who do you think Jan should talk to first? Who do you think is the greedy guts?

Hannah	Turn to **27**
Robert	Turn to **110**
Theo	Turn to **44**
Marta	Turn to **194**
Adam	Turn to **69**

283

Other than it being another sign of Louisa's strange and disconnected management style — she always did have the knack of irritating most people, even when she was trying to be nice — this email doesn't uncover any hidden plots or motives. Still, at least, your hands are no longer green. **Strike off** the codeword CAUL.

You decide to not waste any more time and continue with your original plan, but were you going to see the boss woman (turn to **178**) or the weasely man (turn to **33**)?

284

The actual living worker continues doing her thing — phone calls, amending files, adding to spreadsheets, that sort of thing — but you are distracted by the sound of footsteps coming up the stairs. And then a face appears in the doorway.

'Morning, Hannah. Did you have a good weekend?'

'Hi Marta, yes, and you?'

It's all sounding very polished and not at all real, but it's still interesting watching these two people, who plainly have nothing in common, trying to pretend that they are friends.

'Thanks for the recommendation. I watched 'John Wick' last night. You could have warned me about the dog, Hannah! I can't believe that's your favourite film ever!'

'Oh no, I was just joking,' And Hannah gives a very fake laugh to show that she was, indeed, joking. Or was she? This is excruciating, and you're heartily relieved when Marta waves and heads off towards the kitchen. And only you can see, as you are floating alongside, her face collapse into resting miserable face. Turn to **18**.

285

You hand over the tabloid and watch as the biggest smile spreads over his face. He's already turned to Page 3 and is practically drooling, but before he can vanish to 'entertain himself', his entire form starts to shimmer and boil. Soon, he is a roiling, shapeless mass of colours and then, with a deafening crack of lightening, he is gone. It's safe to say, you weren't expecting pornography to move someone onto the next spectral plane!

Subtract 10 PURGATORY points and **strike off NSFW GHOST** from your Met-A-Ghost list.

Do you want to visit the weaselly man now? If you do, turn to **216**; however, if you've already spied on him, then your next move depends on whether you've ticked the codeword TELEPORTATION. If you have ticked it, turn to **259** and if not, turn to **13**.

286

Halfway down the stairs, the assistant freezes, unlocks the tablet screen, then holds down the Command key while pressing the full stop. It's an escape function and it works! You find yourself tethered and drift with him into the popular Thai restaurant. Although busy, the server sees the company logo on the assistant's temporary name badge and smiles warmly.

'Ah, no Adam today. He is one of our best customers, say hello from me.'

The assistant nods uncertainly, the server's thick Estuary accent proving difficult for him to decipher, but you understand perfectly.

It's too busy for any further conversation and 15 minutes later, you and the assistant return to the office.

There's a moment of confusion and blame-mongering as the CEO wants to start the 'fireside chat' now, rather than wait until after lunch, and despite the food cooling and congealing, that's exactly what happens — she is the boss, after all! Turn to **104**.

287

But you are not alone. Conscripted Ghost has appeared.

'You don't half need some prompting, do you? It's always like this with you new ones. Come on, you've seen words and numbers that the Living haven't, which means they're for you. Things to help you work out why you're here.'

If you were lucky enough in the Bingo icebreaker, you will have seen an incongruous number, and if you succeeded in solving the Treasure Hunt clue, you saw an instruction word. This makes a calculation.

This section number | Instruction word | number

For example, if the instruction word was SUBTRACT and the Bingo number was 120, the calculation would be: 287 − 120 = 167
And you would head to section 167.

If you can't proceed, then you shrug helplessly, hoping that Conscripted Ghost will take pity on you, but he doesn't. With a shake of his head, he sends globules of congealed brain matter across the carpet tiles and vanishes. Turn to **10**.

288

You can wrack your brain all night long, but you're never going to find a reason for Theo to murder Jan! **Add 15 PURGATORY** points, then turn to **150**.

289

Fortunately, for you AND your ex-colleagues, no one is currently using the toilet, so once you've used the white ooze and entered, you have a good look around. The Ladies is uninteresting, but the Gents has a **lemon** in the urinal. You suppose that someone might have put it there as a joke, but then it fades away. Ah-ha! A random object! Just like Conscripted Ghost was talking about. Well, this gives you a bit of a clue, doesn't it? Which word do the objects have in common? Could it be something to do with their colour?

Convert the word into a number, then turn to that section.

If you still haven't got a single idea, then turn to **100**.

290

I have keys but lock no doors
I have space but no rooms
I can enter and escape.
What am I?

'…But whatever the blazes it is,' Clara continues, 'You need to associate it with a person and then you can leave with them. Oh, it's a bit complicated and modern. We didn't really have a lot of electricity in my time and look at it all now!'

Clara sits down heavily on the bottom step, the jolt making her head slide once more onto her chest. Well, you think you know what the answer to the riddle is, but as you still don't remember anyone in the office, this is no use to you at the moment.

Just then, the door opens again and two men enter, barging through you and Clara as they vault upstairs. Clara gives a disgruntled splutter and shouts, 'Oh, the indignity!' which is rather melodramatic but more civilised than your expletive-laden rant. Record that you have met **CLARA**.

Once the dust has settled, you realise that you are alone now, so climb the stairs. You could now go left along the narrow corridor (turn to **32**) or right around the landing (turn to **230**).

291

Theo whistles a jaunty tune, but you can sense that he feels wound up — he may act super-casual but conflict upsets him! He heads straight for the kitchen and roots around in the fridge. Once he's found a stray piece of garlic bread, he stands up but Marta is right behind him.

'That's mine, Theo, and this is getting beyond a joke.'

'I thought it was going spare…'

'No, you didn't. You just didn't care, now give it to me. It's mine!'

Tick **CLUE 10**. And with a mouth full of cold, dry bread, she walks off, leaving Theo in the kitchen, looking bereft. But whether that's because of a lack of food or friends, it's hard to tell.

That might have been an enlightening encounter, but if you're going to get the truth, you need to head back to Robert, And it's clear that you must increase the fear factor!

Have you acquired a pair of phantom shoes? If you have, turn to **153**, but if not, turn to **49**.

292

Hannah goes into a mild trance, then opens the EVIDENCE folder. There's only one document in it — her investigation is going as well as yours! — and with an extra burst of concentration and a squeaky phantom fart, you make her click on the file. Head to **Appendix D** (The 'Evidence' File) at the back of the book but remember **this section number**, as you will return here afterwards.

You stare at the screen, frantically trying to make sense of it, but the facts are undeniable. Hannah is also investigating who gave you the burgundy Tupperware, but why? And what does it mean that Adam, Marta or Louisa had that type? At this point, Hannah gives an irritated shake of her head, then closes the folder, saying, 'Now, where was I?'

Does it really rule the others out, though? Could someone be trying to frame a colleague? Could one of them have borrowed burgundy Tupperware from someone else? Oh, so many unanswered questions! Hannah is now on the phone, talking about SEOs, but have you finished with her? If you've recently ticked the codeword LIMBO and want to try out this new skill, turn to **163**.

If not, then you give up on Hannah and can now check out Marta (turn to **217**), but if you've already done that, then turn to **13**.

293

'Yes, I graduated top of my class, in fact, and my professor still cites my thesis to this day,' says Adam with a faux-humble smile. Marta simply gives him a dead stare until he coughs and walks away. Well, that was a bit awkward!

You then realise that Marta has written the number "**7**" on her card, which is weird, and although you're quite happy to continue with the bingo, too many people are moving around this small space, making both time and the surroundings shift and judder. By the time everything settles again, Louisa is announcing the next activity. Turn to **275**.

294

You've never experienced a fireside chat before, but it seems to be poorly named. There is no fireside, and once Meredith has finished berating Louisa, she marches in and proceeds to simply announce that the London office is being closed. There is a collective gasp and Jan laughs. With an aggrieved tone, she then says that, because of the UK employment laws, there will be redundancy packages or people could relocate to the States.

It's a lot to take in!

'I cannot believe that!' Hannah splutters. 'I've just got my promotion!'

Both you and Conscripted Ghost (who has appeared out of a spectral mist) regard her with pity. She hasn't yet come to terms with her whole lack of existence yet...

'I'm sure you've got plenty of questions, so let's go over everything while we eat. Has anyone ordered lunch?' In the stony silence that follows, Meredith glares at the minions for failing in this one job. Clearly, she wants this to be done and dusted as quick as possible!

'Thank goodness for that,' mutters Conscripted Ghost. 'It's our luck that if they were talking while eating, one of them would choke and then we'd never get rid of them!' You nod in agreement, but maybe you have just remembered something very important that you had to share with this particular spectre. Something that you found when you used a key to open the phantasmagorically locked door...

If so, you were told of a section number to memorise, and you should now **SUBTRACT** that from this section number and *turn immediately* to the new number.

If not, you then spot Hannah, who is frustratedly trying to pass through the door — you really should help her out with some of the phantom laws — but you are more concerned that the window of opportunity for finding your killer is closing fast. You can't investigate an empty office!

But maybe you have found all the clues and learnt all you need to know; it's time to put your money where your mouth is! Turn to **127**.

At first, the atmosphere is slightly awkward. Robert is busily working on a spreadsheet, while Theo has headphones on and is coding. After five minutes though, Robert breaches the silence.

'Did you know that Adam was such a good friend of Ashley? I never got the impression she liked anyone in the office. Obviously not Jan, but no one else either.'

Theo yanks his headphones off and leans back in his chair. It turns out that gossiping about Adam is just the thing that these men can bond over.

'She definitely did not like Adam. The eye rolls she used to give him whenever he spoke in All Hands meetings! Oh no, she thought he was an idiot. Mind you, so do I.'

'So, he's just getting some time out of the office then?'

Theo nods, then sits up with a small gasp.

'Do you think he's winging the four hours off?'

Both say, 'Nah!' at the same time.

'Louisa is there,' points out Robert with a slight blush at the mere mention of her name, 'He wouldn't get away with that, unless he claims that his bike broke down or something.'

Theo nods again, then asks innocently, 'How's the wife and family?' His expression is anything but innocent, so Robert decides to ignore the sly dig and goes back to his spreadsheet.

Theo smirks but just before he puts his headphones back on, he sniffs a couple of times.

'Can you smell chocolate?'

You watch as Robert pretends not to hear and the ghost — Sixties hairstyle and brown miniskirt — continues to chomp on a Walnut Whip right beside Theo's face. It must be off-putting because he gets up, announces that it's time for lunch, then wanders to the kitchen. Behind his back, Robert mutters, 'Brought your own, have you?'

You've got a lot out of this encounter! Tick **CLUES 5, 8 and 10** and record that you've met **BEEHIVE GHOST**, then, being now bored in this office, you decide to leave. Turn to **220**.

296

Pale Ghost beckons you with a weak wave, saying, 'He requested a one-to-one with the boss. It sounds very important.'

And yet, Meredith has gone to fetch a coffee, so Adam is waiting in the lounge area. He's trying to look self-assured, like he talks to the CEO every day, but the frequent, nervous lip-licking is a giveaway. Finally, she returns.

'So, er, Adam, is it? What can I do for you?'

He takes a deep breath in through his nose, then begins.

'It's a challenge to get noticed here; to get rewarded for good work. I've tried raising it in my quarterly reviews, but nothing changes. For example, we had a client presentation that could have led to a significant deal, but despite my PowerPoint being more superior in terms of detail and engagement, Theo was allowed to take lead on it. It simply isn't fair to be overlooked, time and time again.'

After the long, rambling rant ends, Meredith stares at him. You can't tell if she's impressed with his brazenness or dumbfounded that he thinks this is appropriate, but eventually, she says, 'But Theo is the Team Lead…'

Adam stares back, swallows, then stammers, 'Well, yes, right, OK, thanks,' while nodding furiously, and before the blush of pure humiliation can consume him, he walks swiftly to the toilets.

Ouch! That was quite the burn! If you've discovered the TRUTH about Marta, turn now to **84**.

People are still milling around, so there's a chance that the ghosts can notify you of anything interesting happening in their favourite areas — but only if you've **already met them and they are still here**!

| NSFW Ghost | Turn to **241** |
| Charlie | Turn to **79** |

But if they're not an option, then you should investigate what the COO's minion is up to.
Turn to **221**.

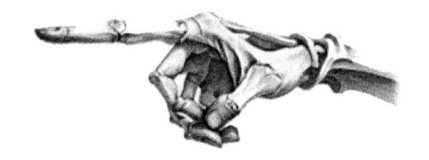

297

With a drop of the good stuff, the door swings open. It is dark beyond, but you can just about make out the stairs ahead. You step down gingerly, wincing as each tread gives an alarming creak and dips, as though under a great weight, despite you being a ghost!

Through the still-open door, the light illuminates a large chamber and, at the bottom of the stairs, a bridge that goes across to the other side. But what's underneath the bridge? The smell answers that question — a stagnant, dank odour that reeks of old aquariums — and now that your eyes have adjusted to the dim light, you can see the thick layer of algae on the surface. It's a moat!

The bridge leads to a gap in the wall opposite. Although the bridge seems rickety and on the verge of collapse, you step onto it, but when you're halfway across, a slight movement in the moat catches your eye. There's something in the water and it's swimming in a slow figure of eight. You watch the undulating algae, wondering if you should just run to the gap, but in these few seconds, you spot two things — a faint glow from the bottom of the moat as though a light is shining down there AND at the far end of the bridge there is a bucket labelled 'FOOD'.

Nothing ventured, nothing gained, so do you want to reach down into the stagnant water to grab the light (turn to **56**) or feed the strange creature with the contents of the bucket (turn to **172**)?

298

What's the rationale here? Do you think that Louisa murdered Marta for the office theft or for being friends with Jan? Either way, it's totally implausible! **Add 10 PURGATORY** points, then turn to **150**.

299

Suddenly, all the anger and despair at your untimely end surges up and explodes out. From Hannah's point of view, it's even more terrifying, as this yellowed, gaunt corpse-like ghost rushes right at her. She screeches a piercing scream and leaps back, but unfortunately, thanks to your earlier rampage, there is a lot of debris on the floor…

She slips, tumbles, grabs for the desk, misses and ends up sprawled on the floor. You loom over her, waiting for her to get up so you can continue shouting at her, but she is strangely still.

When Jan comes running in, yelling, 'What's going on? O mój Boże! Call an ambulance!', you realise that someone is standing next to you.

'I always hated that bloody cactus!'

You turn, mouth gaping in shock. Hannah scowls, wiping the blood that's trickling into her ear, and you know that the shard of plant pot currently protruding from her temple will stay there for eternity.

'I suppose it was quick, but I swear I could feel every millimetre as it went into my brain! Thanks a lot! And for what it's worth, I didn't put the paracetamol in! I just thought that Louisa would

miss her food, realise that you'd taken it and be cross with you. Payback for the interview sabotage!'
Despite feeling guilty about killing her, you still want to know more.

'But why would Louisa put paracetamol in her own food?'

'Well, now I'm not sure that it was even hers. I was doing some investigating after you died, in case someone saw me take the curry out of the fridge, and she wasn't the only one with burgundy Tupperware. I have no idea who brought the curry in and why it was poisoned! So, is this it then? Are we stuck here?'
You nod sheepishly, watching her reaction. And if she thinks this is bad, just wait till she meets Chain-Smoking Ghost!

Despite feeling an obligation to look after Hannah, you become somewhat distracted by a strange sensation in your feet…

It may seem like an odd question at this moment, but do you have a pair of vintage opera glasses? If you do, turn to **176**, but if not — and let's face it, why would you have opera glasses? — then you're probably just imagining things. It's been a long day! Turn to **43**.

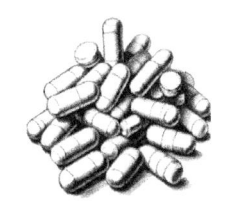

300

Go towards the light! You reach out a hand and grasp the bulb in your desk lamp. Its heat sends your jiggling atoms into overdrive, moving faster and faster until they coordinate into a swirling vortex. It's a beautiful feeling — a delicious warmth seeps throughout your phantom body and your thoughts become pure happiness. Faster and faster, brighter and brighter you go and then…

Poof! You are gone!

Chain-Smoking Ghost watches your departure with jealous eyes, then lights another cigarette.

And if you want to know more about the mutants in the tunnel, keep your eyes peeled for Book 2 in the White-Collar Trilogy…

Appendix

A: What's on the Desk?

A. Monitor	102	**D.** Lamp	99
B. Keyboard	65	**E.** Phone	11
C. Cup	124	**F.** Mouse	78

Now return to the section you were at, which was **15**, **133**, **162**, **181**, or **201**.

B: The Office Floor Plan

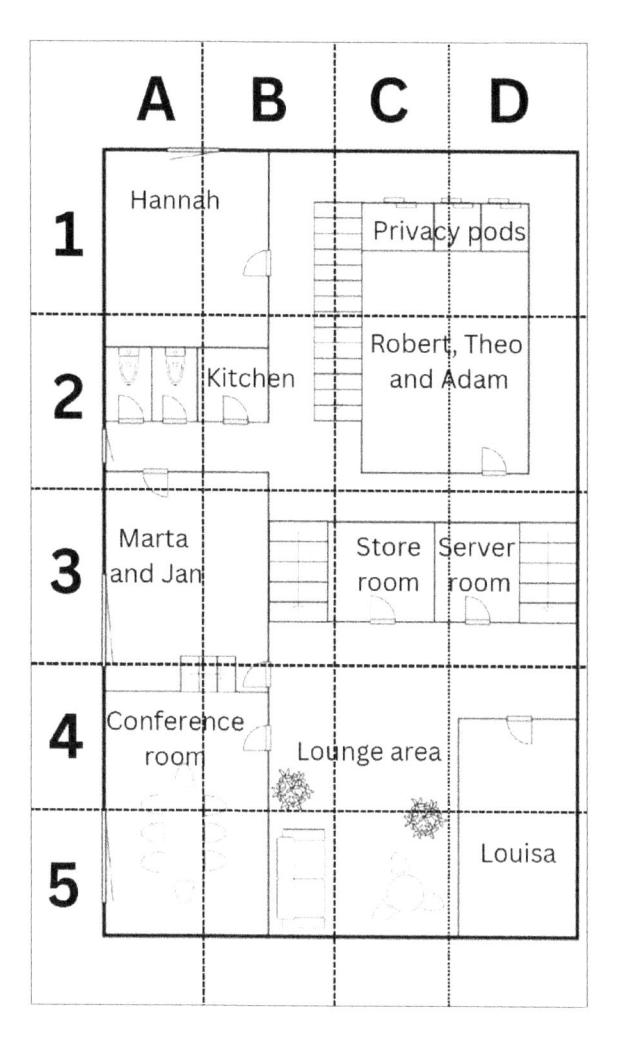

	A	B	C	D
1	Hannah		Privacy pods	
2		Kitchen	Robert, Theo and Adam	
3	Marta and Jan		Store room	Server room
4	Conference room		Lounge area	
5				Louisa

And when you've made your choice, head back to **275**.

C: What the CAUL Reveals…

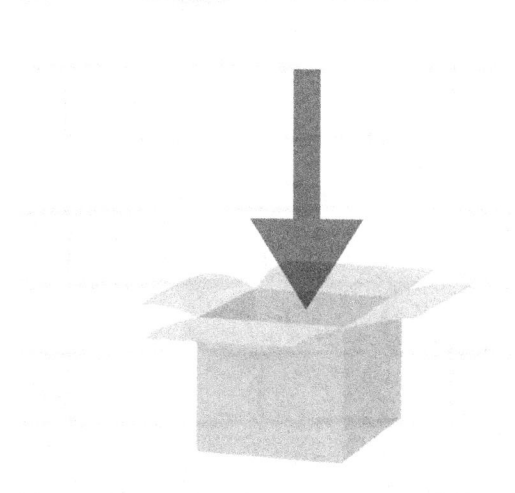

Hmmm. Once you've studied that, you should head back to **124**.

D: The 'Evidence' File

	Tupperware/Lunch habits
Louisa	☑ Burgundy
Robert	☒ Wife gives him leftovers in glass containers
Theo	☒ Eats out (but is allergic to coconut)
Adam	☑ Burgundy (but I haven't seen him use it since Theo joked about it)
Jan	☒ Eats out always
Marta	☑ Burgundy

Tick **CLUE 7**, then return to your previous section, which was either **180** or **292**.

Printed in Great Britain
by Amazon